According to Jennings

Other titles by Anthony Buckeridge in Armada

The Trouble with Jennings
Jennings' Little Hut
Thanks to Jennings
Take Jennings for Instance
Trust Jennings
Jennings in Particular

To
DAVID DAVIS

First published in the U.K. in 1954 by
William Collins Sons & Co. Ltd., London and Glasgow.
This edition was first published in 1968 by
William Collins Sons & Co. Ltd., 14 St. James's Place,
London SW1A 1PF

Printed in Great Britain by
Love & Malcomson Ltd.,
Brighton Road, Redhill, Surrey.

According to to Jennings

Anthony Buckeridge

Armada

CONTENTS

CHAPTER 1

THE MARCH OF PROGRESS

IT WAS during the first few weeks of the Summer Term that the study of inter-planetary flight was taken up with enthusiasm by the seventy-nine boarders of Linbury Court Preparatory School.

According to Jennings, the age of Space Travel was only just around the corner; so in order to help the scientists of the world to skid round this troublesome bend, he and his friend Darbishire lost no time in organising the *Form Three Space-Pilots' League*—a willing band of pioneers, eager to speed up the March of Progress.

There was never any doubt about the success of the movement. In no time at all the space travel craze spread through the school, sweeping away such minor pursuits as the collection of cheese labels and match-box tops, and covering the margins of Latin text books with unlikely-looking drawings of bigger and better rockets.

Scientific societies with high-sounding titles sprang up overnight like mushrooms. Venables and Atkinson organised the *Dormitory 6 Flying Saucer, Space-Ship and Atomic Rocket Development Corporation*: and soon afterwards Binns and Blotwell, the youngest boys in the school, became founder-members of a mysterious group, known as the *Form 1 and Early-Bedders' Guided Missiles Club*, which held secret meetings behind the bootlockers on wet half-holidays.

During out-of-school hours, games of space warfare could be seen—and heard—at every point of the compass. Moon-dwellers in white gym. shoes pursued gangs of flannel-suited Martians across the cricket field; while serious-minded Earthmen scuttled up and down the corridors uttering explosive *"Voom-voom"* noises, or grunting

"Urr-hmmm . . . urr-hmmm" from deep in their throats, as they warmed up the motors of their imaginary rockets.

And yet, despite this widespread enthusiasm, the masters of Linbury Court could find no good word to say for the wave of atomic activity which burst upon their ears at unexpected moments.

The headmaster, Mr. Pemberton-Oakes, curtly refused to allow science fiction magazines to appear on the library shelves; Mr. Carter, the senior assistant, groaned inwardly and "tut-tutted' in despair each time a ten-year-old space mariner spluttered into sight . . . And Mr. Wilkins, who was long-suffering and short-tempered, fumed with disapproval whenever a squadron of Form 3 rockets was heard gargling and snorting at full volume just outside the staff room door.

"That's what I can't understand about masters," Jennings confided to Darbishire, as the two boys stratocruised out of their classroom at the end of school one Monday afternoon. "They're always telling us we ought to do something useful in our spare time; but as soon as we take up a brainy hobby like advanced physics and stuff, they blow up like hydrogen bombs and tick us off for ragging in the corridors."

"The trouble is, they don't seem to see things in the same way as ordinary civilised people, like—well, like you and me," Darbishire replied knowingly. "Not when they grow up, anyway. I dare say Mr. Wilkins was just as keen on all the latest crazes as we are, when he was young."

"Ah, but that was about a hundred years ago," Jennings objected, with wild exaggeration. "You can't expect *us* to get all worked up about magic lanterns and spinning wheels, these days. It's time Old Wilkie brought his ideas up to date. Why, I doubt if he'd even recognise a flying saucer if you brought him one on a plate with a sprig of parsley on the top." He exhaled loudly through his front teeth to apply his air-brakes, and made a skilful three-point landing on the mat at the bottom of the stairs.

Darbishire landed beside him, muttering, *"A-junka-junka-junka-junka,"* to show that he was throttling back his powerful engines; and for some moments they stood on their make-shift runway, shaking their heads sadly over the shortcomings of the staff.

There was a comfortable, easy-going bond of friendship between the two boys, and much of it sprang from the fact that each was quite unlike the other, both in appearance and character.

Jennings was the taller of the two, a friendly-looking boy of eleven with untidy brown hair and a wide-awake look in his eyes. He had about him the restless, eager air of one who acts first and thinks afterwards; of one who must be up and doing in all his waking moments, lest the grass should grow beneath his feet.

Darbishire, on the other hand, would not have worried unduly to find a whole prairie of grassland sprouting beneath his size 3 school sandals; but fortunately his duties as Jennings' right-hand man gave no opportunity for such an alarming state of affairs to occur. For Darbishire was quieter in manner; a loyal follower, but never a leader in the exploits and misadventures of school life. He was fair and curly, with a solemn, rather earnest look about his thin features. Behind his ink-splashed spectacles shone a pair of mild blue eyes which sparkled or clouded with every change in his feelings, as surely as a barometer recording the advent of sunshine or storm.

Presently Jennings said: "Well, let's not bother about Old Wilkie any more. I had enough trouble racking my brains all through his English lesson to last me for some time."

Darbishire looked surprised. "What were you racking them about? I never heard him ask you any questions."

"Oh, no; it wasn't Old Wilkie's fault," Jennings explained. "I was trying to make up my mind between two engine noises. Listen, Darbi: which one sounds more like a space-ship landing on the moon—*Voom-voom-voom* or *Doyng-doyng-doyng?*"

It was a question of some importance, and Darbishire frowned thoughtfully as he tried out both noises with the full force of his lungs.

7

"I don't really know, Jen," he was forced to admit when the echoes had died away. "You see, *my* space-ship doesn't make that sort of noise at all. It just goes *grinkle-grunkle-grunkle* ever so softly, because I've got a secret patent lever I've invented. It's a supersonic gadget: you just give it a flick and off you go . . . Mars, Venus, Mercury—anywhere you like."

He flung out his arm in a sweeping gesture to indicate the outermost limits of space. Then he added: "And you needn't try to pretend that you've got one too, because it's my own special invention, copyright reserved."

Jennings was not impressed. "I bet it's not so good as my super-charged atomic rockets," he said. "I'll challenge you to a race to prove it, if you like. The first one to get up the stairs and into the library, eh?"

"Righto," Darbishire agreed. "We could pretend the library is the moon, and you and I can be rival space-pilots racing to be the first one ever to set foot on its surface—like those chaps in that scientific comic of yours that Mr. Wilkins confiscated."

"Let's get our engines warmed up first then," said Jennings. *"Voom . . . voom . . . voom . . . Doyng . . . doyng . . . doyng . . . Chigga-chigga-chigga!"*

"Grinkle-grunkle-grunkle!" replied Darbishire, setting the mighty motors in action with a deft flick of an imaginary lever.

The hall resounded to the roar of Jennings' rockets as the self-styled space-ships taxied to the starting-point at the bottom of the stairs; but before they could become airborne the door of the nearby staff room was flung open, and Mr. Carter looked out to lodge a protest.

"If you must make that uncouth and horrible hulla-balloo, I'd advise you to go as far away from the staff room as possible," he suggested reasonably. "How on earth do you expect me to add up marks with all the noise of a brass foundry going on just outside the door?"

"Sorry, sir. We were being space-ships," Jennings apologised. "It wasn't meant to sound like a brass foundry, sir. We were just setting off on a race to the moon."

"No doubt; but if inter-planetary travel consists of grunting and snorting through your back teeth, I prefer something a little more old-fashioned," Mr. Carter observed.

Darbishire felt called upon to put in a word for the March of Progress.

"My father says rockets and space-ships are the coming thing, sir. Of course, nowadays we only *pretend* to zoom off to the moon and places. But one day, sir—*who knows*?"

"Who does indeed!" replied Mr. Carter with a smile. He was an agreeable, understanding sort of man in his early thirties. This meant that though still young when judged by grown-up standards, he had already achieved a ripe old age in the eyes of the boys whom he taught. He had been at Linbury Court for some years, and had been teaching boys long enough to have learned a great deal about the way in which their minds worked.

In this he was unlike his colleague, Mr. Wilkins, who at that moment hove into sight at the top of the stairs.

Mr. Wilkins, too, was fond of the boys in his charge, yet the more he saw of them the more bewildered he became by the extraordinary things they chose to do. He was a loud-voiced, burly man, with a brusque manner which concealed a heart of gold. Admittedly, the gold had worn thin in places, and few people were aware of its existence: but at odd and unexpected moments it would break through and dissolve his hasty temper like a watery sun dispelling the blustery March clouds.

At the moment, however, there was no sign of the golden streak, and he clumped down the stairs with the ill-humour of a bull in a cattle truck. As he reached the group in the hall, he heard Mr. Carter say: "All the same, Jennings, I would advise the Form 3 space-pilots and the Dormitory 6 scientific researchers to carry out their work with rather less noise. The staff are growing somewhat jaded by so much inter-planetary flight going on all over the building." He turned to his colleague. "Don't you agree, Wilkins?"

"You never spoke a truer word, Carter," Mr. Wilkins retorted with some heat. "I've just about had enough of the whole stupid business. Every time I turn a corner I bump into silly little boys with smudges of green chalk all over their faces, pretending they're Martians or Mercurians, or some such nonsense."

"Oh, but sir, all planet-dwellers have green faces, didn't you know, sir?" Jennings explained. "If you have a look at that serious comic of mine that you confiscated, it tells you all about it, sir."

"I'll take your word for it," Mr. Wilkins replied. "I don't know much about space travel, I'm glad to say; and if it means going about with a green face, I'd rather stay on earth, thank you very much . . . And another thing: this deafening racket you boys are always creating all over the building . . ."

"Deafening racket, sir?" echoed Jennings, pained at this harsh criticism of his space-craft.

"You know very well what I mean: all this *voom-voom-voom* business, and *chigga-chigga-chigga* nonsense!"

It was the first time that Mr. Wilkins had tried to imitate the sound of a space-ship at full throttle. On the whole he seemed pleased at the success of his mimicry: such a convincing performance was well worth an encore. "And then there's all that meaningless pandemonium of spluttering—*ki-ki-ki-ki-ki-k* at everyone within earshot," he continued, warming to his demonstration. "I tell you, Carter, it's driving me out of my mind."

"Oh, but sir, all those noises *do* mean something," Jennings protested. *"Chigga-chigga-chigga* is what you do when you're ticking over, and . . ."

"I haven't the slightest desire to tick over," Mr. Wilkins pointed out.

"Not *you*, sir. Anyone zooming about in space, I mean. And you only go *ki-ki-ki-ki-ki-k* when you're giving someone a five-second burst of invisible ray-gun fire, sir."

"He means the rays are invisible—not the gun, sir," chimed in Darbishire, who liked to get things right.

Mr. Wilkins' manner displayed a lack of enthusiasm as he turned to the designer of the secret patent lever. "Since you're so good at explaining things, Darbishire, perhaps you can tell me why you find it necessary to scribble blueprints of extraordinary-looking rockets all over the back page of your algebra book."

The inventor blushed. "Sorry, sir: that was just a sort of absent-minded bish, sir."

"Oh, was it! Well, I tell you plainly, you boys, I'm just about reaching the end of my tether over this interplanetary nonsense. And when I'm on duty I'm not going to have the corridors cluttered up with all this space—whatever you call it."

"Cluttered up with space, sir?" Jennings queried.

"You know what I mean," Mr. Wilkins said sharply. "You keep your space games within strict limits, or you'll find Mr. Carter and me far more awkward to deal with than any green-faced monster from the planet Pluto!"

"Yes, sir!"

Obediently they turned and trotted up the stairs. The race to the moon would have to be conducted at walking pace, for supersonic speeds were out of the question while the eagle eye of Mr. Wilkins followed their progress to the library.

As the space-mariners disappeared from view, Mr. Carter turned to his colleague with a smile. "Never mind, Wilkins; these crazes don't last long as a rule. In a week or two they'll have forgotten all about inter-planetary flight, and be absorbed in some quiet and peaceful occupation, such as bird watching, or pressing wild flowers."

By and large, Mr. Carter's prophecy proved to be correct. But could he have foreseen the extraordinary things that were to happen while the space travel hobby was still at its height, it is doubtful whether he would have spoken with such an air of carefree optimism.

The library at Linbury Court was a spacious, book-lined room at the top of the stairs on the first landing. Its main purpose was to provide a quiet retreat where boys with studious tastes could browse amongst the great works of English literature; but when Jennings and Darbishire rocketed in through the door, they found the room being used in the cause of science.

Venables, Temple and Atkinson, three enthusiastic members of the *Dormitory 6 Flying Saucer, Space-Ship and Atomic Rocket Development Corporation*, were sitting in the bay window working out plans for the conquest of space.

"Oh, hullo, Jennings," said Venables, an untidy boy of twelve, whose trailing shoe laces and missing shirt buttons were a constant source of anxiety to the school matron. "We were wondering whether you'd show up. Atkinson's got a super-nimble idea for a new space game. It all takes place on the moon, you see, and . . ."

"And you and Darbi have to try and catch us because

we three are hostile moon-dwellers," Atkinson broke in eagerly.

"They're not called 'moon-dwellers': the proper name is Lunatickians," Jennings corrected. "I know that's right because I had a serious comic—only Old Wilkie confiscated it—which told you all about it in pictures."

The three scientific researchers were clearly impressed by this display of superior knowledge.

"Why Lunatickians?" Venables demanded.

According to Jennings, the term was derived from the Latin word, *luna*, meaning a moon, and *tick*, meaning—er —well, surely they knew what a tick was, didn't they?

"It was a jolly good story, too," he went on hurriedly. "All about a daring space-pilot called Butch Breakaway, who zoomed off to the moon in a secret rocket designed by a famous bald-headed scientist."

"Why not let's bring these characters into our game, then?" suggested Temple. "Jennings could be this Butch chap, and old Darbi could be the scientific geezer with the bald head."

Darbishire's eyes lit up behind his spectacles. Games of space-warfare would seem far more true to life, he thought, if they could model their exploits on real characters—well, as real as a comic strip could make them, anyway!

In his mind's eye he already saw himself as Professor Darbishire, the distinguished designer of space-ships, putting the finishing touches to his latest lunar masterpiece. Suddenly a thought struck him and he asked: "Yes, but look here, you don't *have* to be bald before you can be a famous scientist, do you?"

"No, not nesser-celery," said Jennings. "Anyway, it wouldn't matter whether you were or not, because you'd be wearing a space helmet all the time. You see, there's no air on the moon. That's why the chaps in this comic had to go about with their heads in things like goldfish bowls."

"Golly! They took the fish out first, I suppose?"

Jennings flipped his fingers with impatience. "Don't be

13

such a clodpoll, Darbi! Not *real* gold-fish bowls. They wore these helmets so that they could breathe without air."

"Oh, I see."

There was a pause while this sank in; and then Darbishire said: "But if there's no air on the moon, how do they talk to each other? My father says that sound waves go zooming through the atmosphere at a supersonic speed, and you couldn't possibly hear anyone talking unless there was some air to hear them with."

Jennings perched himself uncomfortably on the edge of the wastepaper basket, and dismissed the problem with a shrug of his shoulders.

"The comic didn't actually say *how* they talked," he admitted. "But there must have been some way, because you could see the things they said written up in little balloons floating over the tops of their heads."

Darbishire frowned thoughtfully. "M'yes, that'd work all right, but only if the balloons were air-tight," he decided. Secretly, he could not quite understand how snatches of conversation could be made to float around in sound-proof containers, but as a newly-appointed scientist he did not like to confess his ignorance.

His gaze wandered round the room and came to rest upon a book-shelf at the far end where a stuffed woodpecker stared beadily out at the world from inside a dome-shaped glass case.

The bird had been presented to the Linbury Court Natural History Society many years before by Lieut-General Sir Melville Merridew, D.S.O., M.C., the school's most distinguished Old Boy, and the gift was always kept in a prominent place in the library in case the General should arrive on one of his unexpected visits.

But it was the glass dome, rather than its feathered tenant, that attracted Darbishire's attention on this occasion.

"That'd make quite a decent space-helmet, wouldn't it?" he remarked—jokingly, of course, for it was unthinkable that anyone should really lay so much as a sticky finger upon the prized exhibit.

14

"Yes, just the job," Jennings agreed, and hurried down the room to inspect the dome at close quarters. "It's just like the ones they had in my comic. I could show you what Butch Breakaway looked like, if it would go on me."

"I shouldn't touch it if I were you," warned Temple. "There'd be a frantic hoo-hah if you dropped it."

"Don't worry; I only want to try it on for size" . . . And without a thought for the consequences, Jennings took hold of the glass case and lifted it down from the shelf.

CHAPTER 2

ATTENTION, ALL SPACE SHIPPING

THE DOME-SHAPED cover rested lightly on its wooden base, and came up quite easily as Jennings lifted it clear of the beady-eyed woodpecker. Then he placed the dome on his head, where it perched awkwardly on his ears like an outsize, transparent bowler hat.

"There you are! How about that for a space-helmet!" he cried triumphantly.

"Jolly good: fits like a glove," was Darbishire's verdict.

"Attention, all space shipping!" Jennings announced in ringing tones. "Here comes the one-and-only famous Butch Breakaway, touching down on the moon in his supersonic radio-controlled space-helmet . . ."

"Captured after a desperate struggle with a moth-eaten woodpecker!" Venables chimed in.

The space pilot turned on the interrupter with the light of battle in his eye. "You shut up, Venables, you're only a hostile Lunatickian." He levelled an imaginary atomic ray-gun at the grinning planet-dweller, and rattled out a fusillade of death-dealing beams from between his clenched teeth.

Venables stood his ground, unharmed by the rays which, in theory, had already reduced him to a heap of radio-active dust.

"It's a rotten space-helmet, if you ask me," he observed critically. "It shouldn't rest on your ears—it's supposed to cover the whole of your face."

He reached up, placed both hands on the top of the dome, and pulled sharply. Down came the space-helmet over Jennings' ears, enveloping his face as far as the point of his chin.

"Ow! Ouch! Mind out, Venables, you gruesome specimen," protested the space-mariner, as the helmet's rim scraped painfully over his nose. But the three Lunatickians were deaf to his protests. They hooted with glee and doubled up in convulsions of laughter.

Not so Jennings! . . . For even as he raised his hand to ease the glass cover, he found that his head was now tightly wedged in the top of the dome.

At once he was overcome by a feeling of panic. Supposing some master came in before he could get it off! . . . Supposing he *couldn't* get it off! . . . Supposing he broke it! . . . Supposing . . . !

"Roll up and see ye famous specimen in ye ancient glass case," chanted Venables, hilarious with mirth, while Temple and Atkinson danced ungainly ballet steps round the unhappy prisoner, making grotesque faces at him through the glass.

But Darbishire had sensed that all was not well.

"What's up?" he asked anxiously.

The answer, faint and muffled, came from behind the wall of glass, and Darbishire cupped his hand to his ear, straining to hear the message.

"What did you say, Jen?" he yelled.

Jennings' lips moved again, mouthing silently through the glass like the image on a television screen when the sound has been switched off.

"Shut up, you chaps!" Darbishire turned impatiently on the cavorting Lunatickians. "I can't hear what he's woffling about. I think he's wedged tight or something!"

"What's up?" asked Darbishire anxiously

Venables was delighted. "I'm not surprised. He's got a bigger head than the woodpecker," he remarked. "He reminds me of a bowl of waxed fruit I saw once in a . . ."

"Help! Help! I'm stuck! Get me out! I'm not fooling, honestly!"

The words were still muffled, but the worried look on the prisoner's face conveyed his meaning as clearly as though some air-tight balloon was floating above the glass case to carry his message to the outside world.

The laughter of the Lunatickians stalled in mid-burst as the gravity of the situation suddenly dawned upon them.

"You can't get it off?" cried Atkinson, aghast.

"Of course I can't," mumbled Jennings. "You don't think I'm half-suffocating in here just for the fun of the thing, do you?"

"Whatever are we going to do? The Head will get in a frantic bate if he finds out we've even touched the wretched thing," Atkinson continued in anxious tones. "We'll *have* to get it off somehow; and without busting it, either."

They took it in turn to try their hands at easing the dome over the worried features of the unhappy space-pilot. But all to no purpose; for each time their efforts were foiled by his tightly wedged ears and the tip of his nose, white and flattened where it pressed against the glass. If only they could have used force, the task would have been simple enough; but this was out of the question, for any rough handling would almost certainly have cracked the delicate dome. What on earth should they do? It was clear that a state of emergency had arisen which called for desperate measures.

"If you ask me, we'll *have* to bust it, if it won't come off before the tea bell goes," Temple observed gloomily some minutes later, after several gingerly attempts had failed to have any effect. "After all, he can't go about for ever with his face in a case; and even if he did, he'd have to have his tea through a straw."

This was such a sensational suggestion that the work of rescue came to a halt while they discussed the possible

18

fate of people doomed to imprisonment in domes . . .
What, for example, would happen when they needed their
hair cut? . . . Would windscreen wipers be advisable in
wet weather? . . . Would Jennings be expected to wear his
school cap when out for a walk? If so, would it balance on
the top, or would it have to be secured in some way?

The debate raged on, each pointless argument becoming more futile and fantastic than the one that had gone
before, until Jennings brought the discussion-group back
to reality with a further agonised appeal.

"Oh, this is ghastly! Help me, somebody! Whatever
am I going to do!"

Atkinson scratched his head in perplexity. Judging from
Jennings' reddening complexion, the atmosphere inside the
dome must be growing sultry, the temperature becoming
uncomfortably warm. Perhaps the glass case, like a diving
helmet, needed a constant supply of fresh air to be pumped
in.

With this in mind, he hurried out of the room in search
of a bicycle-pump with which to construct a make-shift
air-conditioning plant . . . Three seconds later he shot
back again, waving his arms in frantic gestures of warning.

"S-sh! s-sh! Quiet!" he implored in a loud, urgent
whisper. "Mr. Carter and Old Wilkie are beetling up the
stairs! Heading this way, by the looks of it!"

Panic and despair gripped the scientific researchers.

"Petrified paintpots! Hide, Jennings; hide quickly, before they come in!" gasped Darbishire.

The advice, though sound, was not easy to follow, for
the library provided little cover for fugitive spacemen.
With some misgiving, Jennings sidled across to a far
corner of the room and crouched behind a leather armchair.

"Get down lower," urged Venables. "If they see it
bobbing about over the chair there'll be the most ghastly
rumpus."

"Oh, this is frightful," moaned Darbishire, dancing with
agitation. "We should never have let him touch the thing.
My father says . . ."

He stopped abruptly, his hand flying to his mouth in guilty dismay as the tall figures of the two masters appeared in the open doorway.

Mr. Carter was quick to notice the tense atmosphere and unnatural silence.

"It's gone remarkably quiet in here all of a sudden, don't you think, Wilkins?" he remarked.

"It certainly has: and that's usually a sign that somebody's up to some sort of nonsense," his colleague agreed. He stared suspiciously at Darbishire and the three Lunatickians, and noticed that their efforts to appear natural were marred by a tendency to over-act their parts.

Venables stared hard at the ceiling, apparently struck with a sudden admiration for the lampshade; Temple assumed a wide, fatuous smile; Atkinson examined his finger-nails as though he had not seen them for some time; and Darbishire hummed gay snatches of song to show that he hadn't a care in the world.

"All very peculiar," said Mr. Wilkins. "Come along, now, what are you boys doing in here?"

"Nothing—er, well, nothing much, sir: only humming to myself," replied the care-free soloist. "We were just sort of passing the time of day, as you might say, sir."

"I'm delighted to hear it," said Mr. Carter solemnly. He glanced round the room seeking the weak spot in Darbishire's explanation. He soon found it.

"I seem to remember that the last time I came in here, that stuffed woodpecker on the bookcase was protected by a glass cover," he observed.

"Er—woodpecker, sir?" Darbishire queried, playing for time.

"You speak as though you'd never heard of the bird," Mr. Carter said gently.

Darbishire gave him an embarrassed smile. "Oh, yes! I've heard of woodpeckers, sir. Ever so many times, sir. I—er—yes, of course. I see what you mean, sir . . ."

"Don't talk such ridiculous nonsense, Darbishire, you silly little boy," Mr. Wilkins broke in impatiently. "The point is, somebody has removed the glass cover. Come along now—own up. Who was it?"

The Lunatickians remained silent while Darbishire muttered: "Well, we did *touch* it, sir, but not when it was on the bookcase."

Mr. Wilkins looked puzzled. "Where was it, then?"

This was a difficult question to answer without bringing Jennings into the discussion. But Mr. Wilkins was waiting for a reply, and he must be told the truth.

"Well, actually, it was moving about quite a lot, sir— even before we touched it," Darbishire explained. "Part of the time it was near the fireplace, and then it moved . . ."

"I—I—Corwumph!" exploded Mr. Wilkins. "You must be out of your mind, boy. You don't expect me to believe that a glass case would float about in mid-air like a dandelion puff-ball?"

"Oh, no, sir: I didn't mean that. I meant . . ."

"It must have been one of you who moved it; there's no one else in the room," Mr. Wilkins went on angrily. "And that being the case, I shall punish all four of you if I don't get an immediate answer . . . Now then, for the last time, which boy took that glass cover off the bookshelf?"

"Please, sir; it was me, sir."

The answer, distorted and barely audible, came from the far corner of the room, and both masters wheeled round to see the missing dome rising above the back of the armchair, with Jennings' forlorn features encased behind the glass.

"*Jennings!*"

It was well known at Linbury Court that Mr. Wilkins' feelings were easily roused; though it was often bewilderment rather than anger that caused him to fume and threaten like a volcano on the point of eruption.

Here was a case in point. Mr. Wilkins had no desire to put *his* head into a glass case, and he could not for the life of him see why Jennings should feel the urge to do so. Which ever way he looked at it, the thing seemed utterly

21

lacking in reason, and for some moments the master stood staring in speechless amazement.

Mr. Carter was the first to find his voice.

"What on earth are you wearing that thing on your head for, Jennings? Take it off at once, before it gets broken."

Darbishire did his best to explain how matters stood. "He can't, sir. It just won't come."

"We've all been trying, but it's no good, sir," volunteered Atkinson.

"Yes, yes, yes. But what did the silly little boy want to put the thing *on* for!" Mr. Wilkins cried, his voice rising to a squeak of exasperation.

"I—I only wanted to see if it would fit, sir," Jennings mumbled through the glass.

"*Fit?* See if it would fit? You must be off your head, boy," fumed Mr. Wilkins. "Civilised people don't do things like that. You never see Mr. Carter or me going round sticking our heads into glass cases to see if they fit, do you?"

"No, sir. I was just pretending it was a space-helmet, sir."

"I might have known it," snorted Mr. Wilkins. "Can't you boys think of anything else? It's space-ships, space-travel, space-pilots, space-suits, space-boots, from morning till night!"

Mr. Carter grasped the lower edge of the dome and tugged gently upwards. But his efforts were in vain; and it was not until half an hour later, in the dispensary, that Matron succeeded in freeing the chafed and reddened features of the would-be space-pilot. What was even more remarkable was that she carried out this delicate operation without damaging the makeshift helmet.

Jennings was more than grateful. He always got on well with Matron; for she was young and friendly, the sort of person in whom he liked to confide his troubles and problems.

On this occasion she rose even higher in Jennings' estimation, by displaying the kind of sympathy that ought to be shown to people who were unlucky enough to get

22

their heads stuck in space-helmets. She went about her task with no more fuss than if she had been treating a grazed finger, and refrained from making curt comments about the stupidity of his behaviour.

Not so Mr. Wilkins! . . . In the dormitory that evening he had a good deal to say on the subject of inter-planetary flight.

"I'm warning you boys; I've had just about enough of this trumpery tomfoolery," he threatened. "And if there's any more trouble as a result of these ridiculous games, I'll . . . I'll . . . Well, there'd better not *be* any more trouble!"

"No, sir," murmured Dormitory 6 politely; while Jennings sat on his bed massaging his ears with cold cream thoughtfully provided by Matron.

Mr. Wilkins' warning did not go unheeded by the members of the *Form Three Space-Pilots' League*. For nearly a week they rocketed round the building at a slower speed than usual, and reduced the noise of their engines to a low-geared *Brrr . . . Brrr*—at least, whenever Mr. Wilkins was within earshot.

But, unfortunately, a further attack of space-trouble was lurking just around the corner; and it burst upon them in a climax of chaos and confusion on the very afternoon that General Merridew, that most eminent of Old Linburians, chose to pay a visit to his old school.

The headmaster, Mr. Pemberton-Oakes, was not entirely easy in his mind when he saw a letter on the hall table addressed in the General's handwriting. When he opened it and found that his guest was proposing to drop in for an informal chat on the following Wednesday, a slight frown furrowed his forehead, and he remained for some moments deep in thought.

Mr. Pemberton-Oakes was a softly-spoken, rather reserved man in his middle fifties. As a rule he was content to leave much of the routine work of the school in the hands of his staff, though from time to time he would be seized with a desire to make sweeping reforms. Then, he would emerge from his study, glowing with energy, and hustle round the school organising shoe inspections, re-organising the time-table, disorganising meal times, making out new bath lists, appointing new prefects, and sending search parties to look for missing library books. After that he would retire, exhausted, to his study and life would once again resume its normal course.

The headmaster was still wearing his worried frown as he put General Merridew's letter away and went along to the staff room to confide his doubts to his senior assistant.

When Mr. Carter heard the news he said: "General Merridew coming . . . Oh, dear!" in a tone of voice which suggested that he, too, felt a little uncertain about the treat in store.

"Exactly my feelings," Mr. Pemberton-Oakes replied, lowering himself into an armchair. "Naturally, I am always delighted to welcome so distinguished an Old Boy as General Merridew. But between you and me, Carter, he can be a very difficult man to deal with, when the mood takes him—very difficult indeed." He heaved a sigh and shook his head sadly. "If only he would realise that his ideas of how a school should be run are seventy years behind the times!"

Mr. Carter smiled. He knew little about the whims and fancies of elderly generals, but, as always, he took a tolerant view.

"I suppose a hankering for the good old days is quite natural," he told the headmaster. "You'll never get an Old Boy who was here in 1895 to admit that our modern methods are a patch on the way they did things in Queen Victoria's time."

"Quite. And for that reason, Carter, we must spare no effort to see that the boys are on their best behaviour when the General arrives."

"You can leave that to me," said Mr. Wilkins, who had come in during the course of the conversation. "I shall be on duty next Wednesday, so I'll see the place is tidy and the boys are on their toes."

"Thank you, Wilkins. Unfortunately I have to go into

Dunhambury on Wednesday morning, but I shall do my best to be back as soon as possible after lunch. I would suggest that you organise some quiet and peaceful occupation for the boys to pursue, and restrain them from chasing one another round the quad and uttering those ear-splitting noises which seem to be so popular this term."

Mr. Wilkins was as good as his word. Immediately after lunch on the following Wednesday—a half-holiday—he strode round the school barking terse orders about the tidying up of bookshelves and the sweeping-up of pencil-sharpenings.

Binns and Blotwell, who normally wore their socks drooping like concertinas about their ankles and their ties knotted behind their ears, were sent up to their dormitories to make themselves look presentable.

Outside on the quad, Mr. Wilkins found that the latest developments in the conquest of space had started up again after a two-day lull.

Jennings, in his rôle of the dauntless Butch Breakaway, had rounded up the three Lunatickians, and was keeping them covered with an improvised ray-gun, while Darbishire tied them to a tree with a ball of fishing-twine.

"Now, what's going on here?" demanded Mr. Wilkins, walking unharmed through a burst of ray-gun fire. "You boys have no business to be playing these rowdy games. The Head's got an important visitor coming this afternoon." He looked searchingly at Venables, Atkinson and Temple, and noticed the smears of green chalk on their faces. "Go along indoors, and tidy yourselves up, all of you. General Merridew won't want to be confronted with green-faced moon-men every time he turns a corner."

"May we go on with our space-game when we've tidied up, sir?" Jennings inquired.

"Not unless you keep it a lot quieter. I'm not going to have any more of that disgraceful hulla-bulloo that we had to put up with last week."

"We could go to Mars next time, sir. That's a lot quieter than the moon," Darbishire pointed out.

"You're not going to the moon, or Mars, or anywhere

25

else, Darbishire, until you've tidied yourself up. Anyone would think you'd got dressed while the house was on fire, judging by the state your clothes are in."

A truce was declared while the three captives retired indoors to the wash-basins and removed the traces of lunar origin from about their persons. Then Jennings said: "Come on, you chaps. Darbi and I will count a hundred to give you time to get away, and then we'll come after you again in our space-ship."

"But Mr. Wilkins said we were to stop playing," Atkinson demurred.

"No, he didn't. He said we weren't to make a row about it. Get cracking, you Lunatickians! You can take cover anywhere you like inside the building, or on the quad."

Jennings put his hands over his eyes and began to count: "One, two, three, four . . . *wzz* . . . *wzz* . . . ten . . . *wzz* . . . *wzz* . . . twenty . . . *wzz* . . . *wzz* . . . thirty . . . *wzz* . . . *wzz* . . ."

"Hey! That's not fair! You're not counting properly." Venables objected.

"Oh, all right." Jennings started again, more slowly this time: "One . . . two . . . three . . . four . . ."

Outside on the quad a large Rolls Royce purred to a stop, and a tall, imposing, white-haired figure alighted.

Lieut.-General Sir Melville Merridew, D.S.O., M.C., had arrived.

CHAPTER 3

PRISONER IN THE LIBRARY

FROM THE moment that General Merridew set foot in the entrance hall, it was clear that he was not in the sunniest of tempers. He scowled at the maid who opened the front door to him and grunted a surly "H'mph!" at the news that the headmaster had been detained in the local town of Dunhambury, and was not on hand to welcome his guest.

There was, however, a simple reason for the General's ill-humour: he was a man who enjoyed a comfortable snooze after lunch, and his two o'clock arrival at Linbury had given him no chance to indulge in his usual armchair coma.

"If you'll wait in the library, sir, I'll tell Mr. Carter that you're here," said the maid, and scuttled off to the staff room to report the news.

General Merridew frowned at the library furniture and thought, *H'mph!* Leather armchairs, eh! They'd had to make do with hard, wooden benches when *he* had been an inky-fingered third-former back in 1895 . . . What was the modern generation coming to! Too much spoon-feeding, and not enough discipline—that was the trouble . . . Leather armchairs—*H'mph!*

His train of thought jolted to a stop as the door opened and Mr. Carter came in.

"Good-afternoon, General Merridew," he said, and introduced himself with a welcoming smile. "You may remember we've met before; I'm the senior master."

"Good-afternoon to you—though it doesn't show much sign of being a good afternoon *so far*," replied the General ungraciously. He peered hard at Mr. Carter from beneath his proudly beetling eyebrows. "Yes, I remember you; name of Copeland? . . . Campbell? . . . Culpepper? . . . Something like that."

"Carter."

"That's it! Never forget a name or a face." He nodded approvingly at his own remarkable powers of memory. Then he settled himself down on one of the despised armchairs and said: "I'm told the headmaster's not at home."

"He's had to go into Dunhambury; he'll be back soon," Mr. Carter explained.

"H'mph! Pity he didn't think my visit was worth waiting in for. I'm only an old fogey, I suppose, but all the same, I should have thought I was entitled to some consideration when I come back to see my old school."

Mr. Carter sensed the visitor's testy mood and hoped that the headmaster would soon be back to take charge of the difficult guest. "We're delighted to see you again, sir," he said pleasantly, "and I'm sure the boys would appreciate it if you could spare a moment to say a few words to them before you go."

"H'mph! The only reason they want to listen to an old fogey like me is because they expect me to ask for a half-holiday when I've finished," grumbled the General. "Now, back in 1895, Cooper . . ."

"Carter's the name, General."

". . . back in 1895, we didn't get all these half-holidays. We had to work all hours of the day and learn to stand on our own feet. Up at six o'clock in the morning and out on the quad for physical jerks: arms stretch, knees bend, and no monkey business!"

He rose to his feet to demonstrate the exercises that had made him the fine figure of a man that he undoubtedly was . . . But it was too soon after lunch for gymnastics, so he changed his mind and wagged his forefinger at Mr. Carter instead. "Did us all the good in the world, Carpenter. And it's what these youngsters of to-day need to knock the rough corners off them."

"Quite," Mr. Carter agreed, and decided not to bother about his rapidly changing name. "Of course, we still see to it that the boys work hard and play hard, though I expect our modern methods . . ."

"Modern methods—h'mph!" snorted the General. "If you ask me, Codrington, your modern methods, as you call them, are just a lot of poppycock." The word summed up his feelings so exactly that he repeated it: "Poppycock, sir, poppycock! And if you can convince me, Culpepper . . ."

"Carter."

"If you can convince me, Carter, that the youngsters of to-day have the same enterprise and dash that we had back in the nineties, I'll—I'll well, I'll be very surprised."

Tactfully, Mr. Carter persuaded the guest to resume his seat, and then made his escape from the library and hurried away to see whether the headmaster had returned.

There was no doubt that the despised armchairs were very comfortable; and as there was no sign of the headmaster, the General decided that he might, after all, be able to indulge in his customary forty winks.

But not for long! . . . For the number of winks had barely reached double figures when the library door hurtled open as though an explosive charge had been placed behind it, and three breathless boys came clattering into the room at full-tilt.

"Eh! . . . eh! . . . What! . . . what! Good heavens!" spluttered the General jerked back into sudden wakefulness.

They looked like ordinary boys to him, for there was nothing to show that the party now skidding to a halt on the polished floor were three moon-dwellers escaping from the notorious Butch Breakaway and his scientific assistant. The trio skated into the room as far as the table, which they used as a buffer to stop their headlong flight.

Then they saw General Merridew!

"Oh! Oh, my goodness!" gasped Atkinson, no longer a fleeing Lunatickian, but an unhappy small boy who realises that he has just done something unforgivable.

"We—we're terribly sorry, sir; honestly, sir!" stammered Venables, scarlet with guilty shame. "We didn't know there was anyone in here."

"No, we thought the room was empty," added Temple, making the point quite clear.

"H'mph! Nice sort of way to come in, even if you thought the room *was* empty," simmered the General. "We wouldn't have dared to rush about like that in my young days."

"We were playing a game, you see. Someone's chasing us," Venables explained, edging toward the door. "We—er—we'll be going now, if you don't mind, General Merridew."

The Old Boy gave him a penetrating look. "So you know who I am, eh?"

29

"Oh yes, sir. You came down on Sports Day last term and asked for a half-holiday."

"Extremely misguided of me. You probably have far too many half-holidays as it is!"

"Oh, that's all right, sir; we never got it," Temple put in. "The Head thought we'd had quite enough, too."

General Merridew's eyebrows rose in indignation. "You never got it?" he echoed. "Well, that's a nice thing I must say! If I ask for a half-holiday I expect it to be granted, and no shilly-shallying either. Things have come to a pretty pass when an Old Linburian makes a special request and not the slightest attention is paid to it."

He relapsed into an inaudible muttering and the three Lunatickians, after a further spate of apologies, tip-toed out on to the landing, closed the door softly and hurried away to seek a safer refuge in the tuck-box room.

Peace reigned once more in the library. Gradually, the eminent Old Linburian's eyes glazed over, and a moment later he uttered a long, deep sigh like the gentle application of a vacuum-brake . . .

Lieut.-General Sir Melville Merridew, D.S.O., M.C., was having his afternoon nap at last.

Jennings and Darbishire searched for some time without finding any trace of the three Lunactickians. Armed with their atomic ray-gun made out of two cricket-stumps and a pair of garters, and carrying their ball of fishing-line for securing prisoners, the two friends trotted round the school buildings keeping a sharp look-out for Venables and Co.—and an even sharper look-out for Mr. Wilkins.

But all to no purpose; until, just as they were beginning to think that their quarry must be hiding somewhere out of bounds, they met Bromwich, mooching along the corridor all by himself. There was nothing unusual in this, for Bromwich was a lone wolf who often preferred his own company to that of his colleagues in Form 3.

"I say, Bromo, have you seen any hostile moon-dwellers beetling about anywhere?" Jennings greeted him.

"If you mean Venables and all that crush, they went

stonking upstairs like a tribe of hippopotamuses about five minutes ago," Bromwich answered.

"Wacko! Any idea where they were heading for?"

Bromwich ran his fingers through his black hair while he pondered the question. "Yes, come to think of it, I heard Atkinson say they were going to take cover in the library. I gather the scheme was to hide behind the door while you and Darbi went lumbering past."

"Jolly good! Now we've got them! Caught like rats in a trap!" Jennings waved his ray-gun round his head in triumphant glee. "Thanks for telling us, Bromo . . . Come on, Darbi!" . . . And up the stairs he charged hot-foot— as he fondly supposed—on the trail of his quarry.

"How'd it be, Jen, if you dashed in and gave them a five-second burst of space-gun fire, while I stay outside to stop them making a bolt for it?" suggested Darbishire as they raced along the landing.

"Righto! Then we'll . . . No, we won't! I've got a better idea. A really nimble wheeze!" said Jennings, stopping dead in his tracks so suddenly that his friend cannoned into him with some force.

"What are you going to do, then?"

"Lock them in—that's what! . . . The key's sure to be on the outside of the door, so it couldn't be simpler. Then they'll *really* be our prisoners, and they can jolly well stay there till we're graciously pleased to let them out!"

"Oh, how supersonic! This is going to be lobsterous fun." Darbishire pranced from foot to foot and waggled his head from side to side in joyful anticipation.

They hurried along to the library, Darbishire suggesting improvements to the plan as they went. "We could pretend that we don't know they're in there, couldn't we? . . . And you could ask me in a very loud voice if I think they've come this way, and I could say . . ."

"Stop nattering, Darbi, or you'll give the show away," said Jennings sternly. "We'll just creep up and lock the door. Never mind about making speeches until we've got them where we want them."

The library door was shut when they arrived, and the

key, as forecast, was on the outside of the lock. For a moment the two boys stood straining their ears for any sound from within of the hostile Lunatickians.

They heard none; which was not surprising, for Venables, Temple and Atkinson had been safely hidden in the tuck-room for some minutes past, and the sound of General Merridew's peaceful slumbers failed to penetrate the stout oak door.

"Now for it," whispered Jennings . . . He turned the key in the lock!

Then he hammered loudly on the panels and shouted: "Hey, you inside there! You think you're jolly clever skulking in the libe, don't you! Well, now you're jolly well up a gum-tree and you can stay there—and I hope it keeps fine for you!"

General Merridew, roused by the banging, awoke from sleep, and gasped with outraged horror as Jennings' words were wafted through the jamb of the door. But worse was to follow . . .

Outside on the landing, Darbishire put his lips to the key-hole and chanted:

"Ha-ha-ha! . . . Hee-hee-hee! . . . We've locked you in, and pinched the key!"

He broke off, delighted by what seemed to him to be inspired poetry of high quality. "I say, Jen, did you hear that? I made up a poem by accident. I said: Ha-ha-ha . . ."

"All right, I heard," said Jennings shortly. "We'll shove off for a bit and leave them inside, just to show them who's boss around these parts."

The General's moustache bristled in horrified amazement, and he leaped to his feet with a cry of protest. But Jennings and Darbishire merely rocked with laughter at what they mistakenly supposed to be Venables, snorting in mock fury.

Jennings ran off towards the tuck-box room to find someone with whom to share the joke, while Darbishire pocketed the key and made tracks for Dormitory 5, on the far side of the quad. From there, he hoped he would be able to catch a glimpse of the captives through the library windows, and tantalise them to further outbursts of wrath by dangling the key before their eyes.

He trotted along the corridor, happily warbling his accidental poem in a shrill treble:

> "*Ha-ha-ha . . . hee-hee-hee,*
> *We've locked them in and pinched the key.*
> *There they'll stay, till we let them out;*
> *Rumty-tumty-tumty-tout!*"

The last line didn't seem quite right, he thought; but *he* wasn't going to worry! All the same, he would have worried in no uncertain manner, had he known the identity of the prisoner who, even at that moment, stood fuming and fretting on the other side of the library door.

CHAPTER 4

AN OLD BOY REMEMBERS

ALL THE WAY downstairs to the tuck-box room, Jennings chortled with laughter at the thought of Venables, Atkinson and Temple imprisoned in the library. Obviously, his next move must be to find someone to whom he could tell the story; and with this in mind he pranced into the tuck-box room . . . and saw Venables, Atkinson and Temple sitting on the hot pipes in the far corner!

He stopped in mid-prance, his eyes goggling with amazement, and his mouth wide open. It was unthinkable that they could have made their escape by jumping from a first-floor window!

"Fossilised fish-hooks! However did you chaps get down here? I've just locked you in the libe," he gasped.

"That's what *you* thought," grinned Venables.

"We did just look in, as it happened," said Temple, "but we beetled out again at supersonic m.p.h. when we found the old geezer was in there."

33

B

"What old geezer?"

"General Merridew, of course. Old Wilkie told us he was coming this afternoon; don't you remember?"

General Merridew! The room swam before Jennings' eyes. He rocked on his heels and clutched at a stack of tuck-boxes for support.

"What are you looking so fossilised about?" asked Atkinson. "There's no rule about Old Boys not being allowed in the library, is there!"

Jennings found his voice at last.

"Oh, my goodness! This is frantic," he moaned faintly. "Do you know what I've done? . . . I've locked him in!"

"What!"

"Petrified paintpots! Whatever did you want to do a thing like that for? You must be stark, raving cuckoo!" cried Venables, aghast.

"Well, how was I to know? I thought he was you three chaps," Jennings defended himself. "Bromo told me you'd gone into the libe to take cover. And that's not all. I told him he was up a gum-tree, and I hoped it kept fine for him: and after that, Darbishire recited poetry at him through the keyhole."

"Phew! What a ghastly bish. Whatever must he be thinking?" queried Temple.

"Who—Darbishire? He doesn't know yet."

"No; General Merridew, you clodpoll! All very well to tell him he's up a gum-tree, but it's nothing to the gum-tree *you* won't half be up when he gets loose," Temple prophesied gloomily. "If you ask me, Jen, you've gone and landed yourself feet first in the most lobsterous hoo-hah since the Wars of the Roses."

Numb with anxiety they stood staring helplessly at one another for some moments, until the footsteps of the master on duty were heard just outside the door.

Then Jennings pulled himself together with an effort. Heavy in heart, he tottered out of the room to confess his crime to Mr. Wilkins. For this was not a matter that

34

could be lightly overlooked, or passed off with a word of apology . . . *This* was something *frightful*!

Mr. Wilkins thought so, too, when he heard the news.

"You locked him in!" he echoed, unable to believe that anyone in their senses could do anything so stupid.

"Yes, sir: only we didn't mean to. And Darbishire made up a poem by mistake, and recited it through the keyhole by accident, sir."

"But you—you *silly* little boys, what in the name of reason did you do it for?"

"Terribly sorry, sir. We were playing a game you see, and we thought . . ."

"Never mind what you thought," barked Mr. Wilkins. He knew only too well that the General was not the sort of man to bear such an indignity without protest. It really was too bad, considering what the headmaster had said about the boys being on their best behaviour! . . . And then, as a further possibility occurred to him, Mr. Wilkins suddenly burst out: "I say, he's not *still there,* is he?"

"Yes, sir."

"What! Oh, my goodness! Well, don't stand about looking foolish, boy; go and let him out at once."

Jennings gulped. "I can't, sir. Darbishire's gone off with the key in his pocket."

Mr. Wilkins almost danced with frustration.

"I—I—Corwumph!" he spluttered: and, sending Venables hot-foot in pursuit of the key-dangling Darbishire, he hurried away to the library with Jennings trailing unhappily at his heels.

All the way up the stairs, Mr. Wilkins' mind was in a whirl of bewilderment. Of all the nonsensical buffoonery he had ever encountered, he had never before met anything to equal the stupidity of reciting poetry through keyholes to imprisoned generals. Why, he asked himself bitterly, did these things always have to happen when *he* was on duty!

Any hope that the General might be bearing his imprisonment with calmness and military fortitude was dispelled by the shouts and bangs which greeted Mr. Wilkins while he was still some distance from the room.

"Hey! Open this door! . . . What is the meaning of this outrage!" came in angry tones from within.

"It's all right, General Merridew," Mr. Wilkins assured him through the panels. "If you wouldn't mind waiting just a few moments . . ."

"I'm not waiting *any* moments. Open this door at once, d'you hear!"

"Yes, yes, of course. The only trouble is . . ."

How on earth could he explain? Mr. Wilkins wrung his hands in despair and turned sharply on the luckless Jennings. "You really are incredibly stupid. You must be off your head," he said loudly.

"What's that? Must be off my head! How dare you, sir!" came in furious accents from the other side of the door.

"No, no, no, not *you*, General. I was talking to a boy."

"Fine time to start chatting to boys, with me locked in here like a wretched jail-bird," stormed the distinguished guest. "This sort of thing didn't happen in 1895, I'll have you know."

Regardless of the crease in his trousers, Mr. Wilkins knelt down and applied his lips to the keyhole, determined to explain the position at all costs.

"Please accept my deepest apologies, General Merridew," he began. "Something most unfortunate has occurred, and I must ask you to be patient for just a few moments longer. I have sent a boy to retrieve the key from Darbishire, and as soon as he returns . . ."

"You've sent him to Derbyshire! But, bless my soul, that's two hundred miles away. He won't be back before to-morrow."

"No, no: not the county—a boy of that name. I'm expecting the key any minute now."

Mr. Carter was humming to himself as he made his way back to the library from the headmaster's study. Mr. Pemberton-Oakes had not yet returned from Dunhambury; but as it seemed unlikely that he would be away much longer, Mr. Carter decided to go and inform the honoured guest that the time of waiting was almost passed.

With this in mind he turned into the corridor leading to the library . . . And at once the humming died on his lips and gave place to a gasp of surprise at the sight of Mr. Wilkins kneeling in the corridor making a speech through the jamb of the library door.

"Well, really, Wilkins!" he exclaimed. "What on earth are you doing? Do you realise that General Merridew is in there, waiting to see the Head?"

"You don't have to tell *me* that, Carter," retorted Mr. Wilkins, breaking off his speech and turning on his colleague with some heat. "This wretched boy has locked him in; and so far as I can make out, that half-witted Darbishire has gone off with the key after giving a poetry recital through the keyhole."

"It wasn't much of a poem, really, sir," said Jennings, who liked to get things right. "All he said was: 'Ha-ha-ha . . .' "

"Be quiet, boy: I don't care if he recited the *Complete Works of Shakespeare*—the damage is done now."

The situation was bad enough in all conscience, but it became worse a moment later when Venables arrived with the news that Darbishire and the key were nowhere to be found.

"Whatever shall we do, Carter?" groaned Mr. Wilkins, as renewed thumps and cries of protest sounded from within.

Mr. Carter sized up the state of affairs and made a quick decision. The library was on the first floor, so the General could hardly be expected to undertake an airborne leap on to the quad below. A ladder was the obvious solution: by this means the two masters, armed with a screw-driver, could climb in through the window, remove the lock from the inside of the door, and set the thumping prisoner free.

"Good idea, Carter," said Mr. Wilkins, as his colleague outlined the plan. "There's a ladder behind the gymna-

37

sium. Come and give me a hand, and we'll have him out in no time."

With a brief word of explanation to the imprisoned guest, they hurried away to put their plan into operation. Venables followed, determined not to miss the excitement, and Jennings was left alone outside the door.

He was not alone for long: for no sooner had the masters disappeared on their errand of mercy than a light footstep was heard at the far end of the corridor, and C. E. J. Darbishire, in person, came skipping into view, still chanting snatches of his immortal verse in a tuneless treble.

"Ha-ha-ha . . . Hee-hee-hee,
We've locked them in and pinched the key,"

he warbled.

It was clear that Darbishire was not abreast of recent developments, and Jennings lost no time in bringing him up to date.

"You great, addle-pated clodpoll, Darbishire! Where have you been?" he demanded.

"I've been up in Dorm. 5, trying to have a look at them through the window, but I couldn't see properly."

"Well, you might have told me you were going. Venables has been looking for you all over the place."

"Venables has? Don't be crazy, Jen! How could he, when he's locked up in there?" Darbishire retorted, pointing a finger at the library door. "Why, as a matter of fact . . ."

He broke off as the General's indignant tones rang out in a renewed burst of protest. "Hey! You outside there, whoever you are! How much longer do you expect me to go on waiting for someone to unlock this door?"

A puzzled expression spread over Darbishire's features.

"That doesn't sound like Venables," he said.

"You never spoke a truer word," Jennings replied. "Hand over that key We've got enough trouble coming our way to last us for the rest of the term."

"But who is it?" demanded Darbishire, as Jennings took the key and inserted it in the lock.

"Never mind: you'll know soon enough."

A moment later the key turned in the lock, the door swung open and the two boys took a step backwards, as General Merridew stepped wrathfully over the threshold, demanding explanations and uttering threats all in the same breath.

For some moments the General's anger continued to simmer like a slowly cooling cauldron, while Jennings and Darbishire hopped from foot to foot in embarrassment, and mumbled a jumble of explanation and apology.

"We're terribly sorry we locked you in, sir. It was all a frantic bish—er, a mistake, I should say," Jennings volunteered. "We thought you were three friends of ours."

"You thought I was . . . !! Do I *look* like three friends of yours?" demanded the General, puzzled by what seemed a queer way of showing friendship.

"No, no, not really, sir. We were playing a game, and our friends were hostile so we had to chase them with invisible ray-guns, sir."

"He means the rays were invisible—not the guns," Darbishire added so that there should be no doubt about the matter. "We were on the moon, you see, sir."

"On the moon!"

The Old Boy's eyebrows shot up like window blinds as he sought to make sense of these fantastic explanations.

"Yes, sir; only not *really*, of course," Darbishire went on with a little nervous laugh. "Jennings was being Butch Breakaway, you see: but that's not his proper name, of course—any more than I'm really a bald-headed scientist."

It had not occurred to the General that the curly-headed figure before him *was* a bald-headed scientist. So he exhaled gustily through his moustache, and awaited further details with what patience he could muster.

"Well, you see, I'm supposed to be Professor Darbishire, the famous inventor of *Lunar Space-Ship Mark 1*; and according to Jennings there's no air around these parts, so we have to talk to each other in little balloons."

39

"And we really ought to be wearing space-helmets too, sir, only there was a bit of a hoo-hah the last time we did that," Jennings added.

He noticed that General Merridew was still looking rather puzzled, so in order to make the explanation clear he prattled on for some minutes, describing the rules of space warfare in detail. He told him about Darbishire's patent secret lever, about the mythical Butch Breakaway, and the fleeing Lunatickians.

And as the story was unfolded, a curious change came over the most eminent of Old Linburians. After a while he stopped fuming and *h'mph*-ing; his beetling brows descended to their normal level, and he listened to the apologetic prattler with interest—almost with sympathy.

Two reasons accounted for this change in the General's feelings. First he had, after all, been able to snatch some thirty-five of his usual forty winks; and this in itself was enough to restore his spirits and enable him to face the rest of the day with his customary vigour. But, more important still, there was something about the taller of the two boys that reminded the General of what he himself must have looked like at that age. And the thought sent his mind racing back more than half a century to the days when he had been as lively a third-former as ever harassed a long-suffering schoolmaster.

The more he thought of it, the more it seemed to him that the games he had played then were not so very different from the games that these boys were playing now . . . Of course, they hadn't had atomic rockets in 1895—they'd had to make do with balloons. All the same, lunar expeditions had been just as popular in his day when based on the books of Jules Verne, as they seemed to be now, when borrowed from some scientific comic strip.

"Journey to the moon, eh!" he murmured wistfully, when Jennings' tale had faltered to a close. "Well, well, well! How it takes me back. How clearly I remember those lunar expeditions we used to plan seventy years ago!"

"You—you mean *you* played those games too, sir!"

40

gasped Jennings, unable to believe his ears. He was astounded to learn that space travel was not so up-to-date as he had supposed; but he was even more astounded at the thought of the elderly General Merridew charging round the school at full-tilt, in imitation of a Nineteenth Century space-traveller.

"Of course we played them. I wasn't always an old man with a white moustache," replied the General, chuckling to himself. "We took our ideas from that French writer-fellow who was so good at turning out stories of that sort . . . You know the ones—*Twenty Thousand Leagues Under the Sea* . . . *Round the World in Eighty Days* . . . *Five Weeks in a Balloon* . . . *Journey from the Earth to the Moon*. We had them all in the school library, back in the 'nineties."

"They're still there, sir," Darbishire told him. "And I should think they're the same copies that you had, judging by the state they're in."

He trotted in through the library door and opened a cupboard stacked high with dog-eared, mouldering books. They were all too old and dilapidated for general use, and were kept in the cupboard for the benefit of anyone who wanted to browse amongst the juvenile literature of a bygone generation. Torn, coverless, with yellowing pages, they still held a strong appeal for Darbishire who would often spend a wet half-holiday thumbing his way through the out-dated volumes.

He ran his eye down the stack of books, selected a title, and then skipped back into the corridor where he passed the volume across for their guest's inspection.

The Old Boy could not have been more surprised and delighted if Darbishire had presented him with the original manuscript of the Doomsday Book.

"*Journey from the Earth to the Moon* by Jules Verne," he breathed, screwing up his eyes to decipher the worn lettering on the spine of the book. "Why, I believe this is the very same copy I used to read under the desk during algebra lessons."

He flicked his way through the pages and paused with

41

a wistful longing at the sight of a large ink blot on page thirty-seven, which he now remembered having made over sixty years before, through closing the book too quickly at the approach of a master.

"Well, well: I never thought I'd meet this old friend again. How it all takes me back!"

His change of mood was complete. No longer a peppery old soldier, but once again, in his imagination, an inky-fingered third-former having the time of his life at the expense of some peppery old schoolmaster.

"Ah, those were the days!" he sighed longingly. "And now I come to think of it, Jorkins . . . Jevons—or whatever your name is—I seem to remember that *our* lunar expeditions always used to finish up with a chase of some sort. Lots of dashing about and taking prisoners . . . Always led to trouble."

"So will ours, this time," Jennings said sadly. "What with our locking you in, and everything."

General Merridew laughed heartily.

"You needn't go on apologising about *that*," he replied. "It was nothing—a mere bagatelle. Why, now I come to think of it, I remember shutting our Latin master in this very room, way back in '97."

The two boys stared at him, wide-eyed with surprise. It was difficult to imagine this white-haired patriarch in the rôle of a ten-year-old practical joker.

"Oh yes, I was quite a gay spark in those days," the General went on, as old memories flooded back into his mind. "Now what was the master's name? . . . Old chap with a beard: began with a B . . . Blenkinsop? . . . Bundleberry? . . . Bottlewell?—I don't know! Anyway, he was sitting in the library just as I was a few minutes ago, when I suddenly felt an overpowering urge to pull his leg."

He had not given the incident a thought for over half a century; but now, as he recounted the story, he could recall every detail of that far-off afternoon when he had tied one end of a ball of string round the knob of the library door. Then, he had stretched the string across the landing, over the banisters, and secured it to the school bell at the foot of the stairs on the floor below . . . After that, he had knocked on the library door.

"And what happened then, sir?" asked Jennings eagerly.

"Well, Old Bottleworthy . . . Boltingrass—or whatever his name was, tried to open it. And he couldn't, of course, because—ha-ha-ha—because the handle was tied. All he did was to ring the bell downstairs in the hall. Ho-ho-ho!"

General Merridew paused to regain his breath, his face a delicate shade of purple and tears of laughter streaming down his cheeks. "Oh, dear, oh, dear! The more he tugged the louder the bell rang, and he still couldn't open the door more than a—ha-ha-ha—more than a couple of inches."

Jennings and Darbishire felt a little uncertain about joining in the General's merriment. It was all very well for him to speak lightly of imprisoning people in libraries, but *he* had not sounded so pleased when it had happened to him.

"This door opens inwards, you see," the General said with his hand on the knob. "I could show you how it worked if only I had a long piece of string."

With some hesitation Darbishire produced from his pocket the roll of fishing line with which he had planned to tie up any stray Lunatickians whom he might be lucky enough to capture. "Would this do, sir?" he asked.

"Capital! The very thing, Devonshire . . . Dorsetshire—or whatever your name is."

The General took the line, tied one end to the door which he closed behind him, and then paid out the roll across the corridor and over the banister rail. After that he led the way downstairs, paying out the line as he went, and feeling as though seventy years had dropped off his shoulders in the space of a few seconds.

"Still got the same old school bell hanging in the hall, I see," he observed, nodding approvingly at the heavy brass object suspended from a bracket on the wall.

It was an old-fashioned bell, seldom used now that the school had been equipped with an up-to-date electrical device which shrilled its message to the farthest corners of the building; but the old bell remained as an ornamental reminder of a more leisurely age.

On the top was a brass ring to which the bell rope was attached: one strong pull on the rope would start the whole instrument swinging to and fro, and set the clapper beating against the sides with a resounding clang.

General Merridew slipped the end of the fishing-line through the brass ring and made it fast with a clove hitch.

"There you are," he beamed. "Anyone trying to open the library door will be astonished to find himself ringing a peal on the old bell. Of course, we really ought to have some unsuspecting person inside the library for the trick to work properly. However, we'll pretend there's someone there, just for the sake of my little demonstration."

The General was more fortunate than he realised. Though he had no means of knowing it, an unsuspecting person in the shape of Mr. Wilkins was, at that moment, preparing to climb the ladder he had set up against the library window, intent upon his errand of liberation.

CHAPTER 5

MR. WILKINS RINGS THE BELL

THE LADDER was a heavy one, and Mr. Carter and Mr. Wilkins had some difficulty in manhandling it across the quad and setting it up against the library window.

As soon as it was in position, Mr. Carter produced a pocket screw-driver which he handed to his colleague and motioned him to climb aloft.

"Up you go, Wilkins. I'll keep the foot of the ladder steady for you."

Panting and gasping though he was, Mr. Wilkins still had enough breath left to put in a lively protest.

"Well, I like that! Why do *I* have to go up first? The Old Boy will be dancing with rage by this time, and if I've got to take the full onslaught . . ."

"Oh, go *on*, Wilkins! He's been shut up for quite a long time already. Goodness knows what'll happen if he isn't let out soon."

"All right, all right, I'm going. Just give me a chance to get my breath back," grumbled Mr. Wilkins, stepping on to the ladder.

As he climbed, he continued to mutter criticism of his colleague in a mumbling undertone. "All very well for some people to find themselves nice safe jobs at ground level, but if the Old Boy goes into the attack while I'm still ladder-borne . . ."

By now he had reached the big bay window on the first floor. He raised the sash and peered inside "General Merridew! . . . General Merridew!" he called.

Slowly, a look of bewilderment spread over his features, and he called down to his colleague at the foot of the ladder: "I say, Carter, he's gone . . . Vanished! . . . Disappeared! The room's empty."

"Nonsense," retorted Mr. Carter. "You don't expect me to believe he's flown up the chimney like Father Christmas, do you? Perhaps he's fallen asleep in one of the armchairs."

"No, he hasn't I tell you. Come up here and see for yourself."

Mr. Wilkins opened the window to its full extent and climbed inside. He was joined a few moments later by Mr. Carter, and for some seconds the two masters stared round the room in surprise.

There was no doubt about it—the guest had departed. Obviously, someone had forestalled them by producing the key; and Mr. Wilkins, still clutching his screw-driver, hurried across to the door to pursue his investigations in the corridor . . . But the door wouldn't open; which was odd, because a quick glance was enough to show that it was not locked.

He took a fresh grip on the handle and tugged again. The door moved a full two inches, but in spite of his efforts it refused to open any wider.

"That's funny; it seems to be stuck," the master observed, agitating the door to and fro with some force. . . . And as he did so, the faint musical tinkle of the school bell was wafted up the stairs.

"Now, who on earth . . . Did you hear that, Carter?" He let go of the handle and listened. But now there was nothing to hear, for the ringing ceased as soon as the door came to rest.

"Never mind about the bell; try and get the door open," Mr. Carter advised; and Mr. Wilkins returned to his task with a vigour that set the clapper clanging against the bell as loudly as the curfew tolling the knell of parting day.

"It won't open any wider. I can't think what's happened," fumed Mr. Wilkins: and in a burst of frustration he added: "And what's more, I'd like to know who's fooling about with that bell, downstairs. I'll have a thing or two to say to him when I find out who it is."

Quietly, Mr. Carter said: "I rather think it's you, Wilkins."

"*Me!* Don't be ridiculous! How can it be me?"

"Hasn't it struck you that the harder you tug at the door the louder the bell rings?"

Mr. Wilkins gazed at his colleague in astonishment. Then he carried out a few simple experiments with the door handle and found that the theory was perfectly correct.

"But . . . but . . . I . . . I . . . It's too fantastic for words, Carter. Here we come running with ladders to liberate the General, only to find he's gone and we can't get ourselves out. And, as if that wasn't enough, some witless imbecile chooses this particular moment to start playing ducks and drakes with the school bell. What must General Merridew be thinking?"

Angry now, Mr. Wilkins heaved at the door-handle like the anchor-man of a tug-o'-war team, muttering to himself to the accompaniment of a musical peal from the floor below.

"If I could ... (*Clang!*) ... only get ... (*Cling!*) ...; this wretched door open ... (*Clong!*)"

Mr. Wilkins' prowess as a bell-ringer had not passed unnoticed on the ground floor. At the first tinkle, General Merridew opened his eyes wide in surprise; and as soon as he had recovered from the shock, he stood beaming and smiling with delight at this unsuspected climax to his little joke.

Not so Jennings! ... Recent events had given him little time to wonder how the masters had been faring with their ladder; but now it was as though the jangling of the clapper was also ringing a bell in his mind. With growing apprehension he beckoned to Darbishire to leave the General and follow up the stairs.

When the boys reached the library, they were neither of them sure what to do next, for they had no wish to offend their distinguished guest on the one hand, or Mr. Wilkins on the other.

Their problem was solved when Mr. Carter heard them discussing the situation in low whispers outside the library door.

"Is that you, Jennings?" he called.

"Yes, sir."

"What are you doing out there?"

"Nothing, sir. Or rather, we're only listening to you and Mr. Wilkins ringing the bell, sir."

"I ... I ... Corwumph!" fumed the unwilling campanologist. "Open this door at once, you silly little boy."

"Yes, sir."

Jennings cut the fishing line with his penknife. Then, for the second time that afternoon, both boys took a defensive step backwards as an irate figure came hurtling out of the library with the force of a fighter-pilot on an ejector-seat.

"Jennings! ... Darbishire! ... What on earth is the meaning of this tomfoolery!" thundered Mr. Wilkins. "First you shut General Merridew up in here, and then you play the same stupid trick on Mr. Carter and me."

47

"Oh, no, we didn't, honestly, sir. It was an accident both times. You see, sir, what happened was . . ."

Mr. Carter decided that the explanation could afford to wait until a more convenient moment. The immediate task, obviously, was to find the honoured guest.

"Do you know where the General is now, Jennings?" he inquired.

"Oh yes, sir. We've only just left him," Jennings answered. "I'll take you to him, if you like, sir."

He was about to lead the way down the stairs, when the tall figure of the headmaster appeared round the corner at the far end of the corridor. He had returned somewhat later than he had expected, and was a little worried by the thought that his guest had been kept waiting.

"Are, there you are, Carter! I understand that General Merridew has already arrived," he said, as he reached the group outside the library door.

"Yes, that's right; he certainly has."

"Then why has no one brought him along to my study?"

"It's all the fault of these two boys," Mr. Wilkins broke in. "They shut Carter and me up in the library."

"They did *what!*"

Mr. Pemberton-Oakes was a man who seldom betrayed his feelings, but now he blinked three times, convinced that his powers of hearing had deceived him.

"Oh, but, sir . . ."

"Be quiet, Jennings," the headmaster said, in tones as frigid as an ice-cube. "Seldom in the course of my professional career have I encountered such wilful disobedience. I can only assume that such outrageous conduct is the result of your reading that—ah—that so-called comic paper, which I was thankful to observe Mr. Wilkins confiscated at the first opportunity." He grasped the lapels of his jacket and took up the stance he always assumed when about to lecture the school upon the subject of good behaviour. "The influence of the strip cartoon, as I have frequently remarked, is one which cannot but cause con-

48

sternation in the minds of those whose duty it is to supervise the literary tastes of the rising generation . . ."

It seemed to Mr. Carter that this was not a good moment for a long-winded address on the trends of juvenile fiction. He brought the topic back to the point of discussion by asking: "Just why did you lock us in, Jennings?"

"But it wasn't us who did it; honestly, sir."

"Nonsense! It must have been you. There's no one else about," Mr. Wilkins broke in, pointing up and down the corridor to prove his argument.

The headmaster nodded in agreement. "Exactly. It's quite obvious that you two boys are responsible. I regard this as an extremely serious matter, and I intend to punish the pair of you with the utmost severity."

Jennings wrung his hands in despair. "But we really, honestly didn't shut them in, sir," he pleaded, distressed almost to tears that no one would give him a chance to explain.

"Don't be ridiculous, boy," snapped Mr. Wilkins. "If you didn't shut us in, *who did*?"

"I'm afraid *I* did."

The deep voice came from just behind them, and the whole party wheeled round in surprise to find General Merridew standing at the top of the stairs. He was blowing self-consciously through his moustache and wearing a slightly embarrassed smile.

The effect upon the staff was considerable.

"General Merridew!" gasped the headmaster.

"I . . . I . . . Good heavens!" stammered Mr. Wilkins.

"I didn't hear you come up, General," said Mr. Carter.

"Come to face the music like an old soldier," said the most distinguished of all Old Linburians. "Always owned up to my misdeeds when I was a boy here, and I'm not afraid to do it now . . .Well, Headmaster, what's the punishment? Six of the best, eh?"

Mr. Pemberton-Oakes remained outwardly calm; not even the flicker of an eyelid betrayed the turmoil that was going on in his mind. There must be some mistake, he told himself: his guest could not seriously mean what he said.

49

"I don't think you quite understand, General. I was inquiring into the matter of who shut these masters in the library. Naturally I can hardly suppose that you had anything to do with such an—ah—such an irresponsible act."

"Oh, yes I did."

One does not doubt the word of eminent generals. Mr. Pemberton-Oakes stood regarding his guest with a puzzled smile, completely at a loss to understand what lay behind this incredible confession. And, indeed, his bewilderment was natural: for there was nothing to show that a change of heart had come upon the General as the result of his meeting with the two boys.

"All my fault. Better try to explain," the General admitted with a wan smile. "I don't quite know how it happened, but talking to these lads here about the sort of games I used to play when I was their age, took me right back to the time when I was an inky-fingered young scallywag myself."

It was not an easy matter to explain; and though the General did his best, the masters could not quite follow the rambling story about the long-forgotten Mr. Blundell-worthy . . . Or was it Blenkingrass? . . . Perhaps it was Bottleberry?—not that it mattered much!

What *did* matter was that the General was now in the sunniest of tempers, and feeling grateful to the two youngsters who had helped him to recapture a brief moment of his boyhood which he feared had been lost for ever.

He was delighted, too, that his little prank still worked as neatly as it had done in 1897. It might even be said to work better; for this time he had caught not one victim, but *two*!

"My apologies, gentlemen," he finished up, turning to his victims with a smile. "Naturally, I had no idea you were in the library at the time."

"No, no; not at all. Quite understandable," murmured Mr. Wilkins, still feeling a little dazed. "After all, boys will be boys, what!"

Jennings and Darbishire exchanged glances. Mr. Wilkins

had not sounded so forgiving when he thought *they* had been the cause of the trouble.

The General was smiling broadly. "Boys will be boys, eh!" he echoed. "Very true, very true, though it took these young rascals to remind me of the fact. And I dare say they're still as keen on an extra half-holiday as we were in the 'nineties, eh?"

"Oh yes, sir; rather, sir," said Jennings.

"Might even make it a *whole* holiday to make up for the one they missed last term, eh, Headmaster!"

Mr. Pemberton-Oakes pulled himself together with an effort. He had seldom seen the General in such an expansive mood; perhaps the boys' efforts to entertain him had not been so unsuccessful after all.

"A whole holiday? . . . H'm: I shall have to think about it. Meanwhile, General, perhaps you'll come along to the drawing-room for tea," he remarked pleasantly, with a gesture that included the two masters in the invitation.

Jennings and Darbishire stood watching as the honoured guest was led away to the drawing-room, his brusque manner now mellowed by sentiment.

"I remember a funny thing happening here one day in '96," he was saying as he accompanied his host along the corridor. "This master I was telling you about, old Mr. Birtletop . . . Blinkinghorn—I wish I could remember the old boy's name. Anyway, he had a long white beard; and one day he got some ink on his fingers . . ." His voice died away in the distance.

Darbishire heaved a sigh of relief. "Phew! I thought we were in for the most frantic hoo-hah, didn't you, Jen?"

"You just can't tell with grown-ups," Jennings answered with a shake of his head. "They make up rules and then break them, just because they feel like it. Now if it really *had* been us who'd caused all the rumpus, the Head would have blown up like a hydrogen bomb. But just because it turned out to be the old General's fault . . ."

He left the sentence unfinished: his feelings were too deep for words.

CHAPTER 6

INDOOR CRICKET

THERE CAN be no doubt that General Merridew enjoyed his visit to his old school. For not only did he ask for a whole holiday to be granted the following week, but, in a further burst of generosity, he invited the first and second cricket elevens to celebrate the occasion by watching the day's play in a county match at Dunhambury.

The market town of Dunhambury lay three miles west of Linbury Court as the crow flies, and nearly twice the distance when measured by the bus route. In point of fact, crows seldom made the journey non-stop, but had they wished to do so any fast-flying crow could easily have out-distanced the local bus: for the hilly road wound over the South Downs, where steep gradients reduced the average speed to a leisurely twelve m.p.h.

The cricket ground at Dunhambury was small; so small that county matches were not played there regularly. Once or twice each season, however, the county team would forsake its more spacious grounds and journey to Dunhambury for three days of cricket in delightful surroundings.

A fixture had been arranged for the middle of June; and thus it was that General Merridew, though he could not attend in person, was able to invite the Linbury boys to watch the second day's play in a match between Sussex and the M.C.C.

The news of the invitation was received with wild enthusiasm when a notice to this effect was pinned up in the hall some days after the guest had departed. The tidings spread from lip to lip, and within a few minutes the corridors resounded to the clatter of juvenile footwear, as boys converged upon the notice-board from all direc-

52

tions. In matters like this, it was vital to make sure that the news was no idle rumour or heartless hoax.

Jennings was oiling his cricket bat in the narrowest part of the corridor, when the stampede to the notice-board warned him that something sensational was afoot.

First, Venables came stumbling round the corner at full-tilt, cannoning into Jennings and sending the uncorked bottle of bat-oil slithering along the linoleum with an accidental kick. As it rolled over and over, it left in its wake a winding river of oil which spread stickily in all directions.

"You clumsy clodpoll, Venables!" stormed Jennings. "Look what you've done—spilt the whole bottle *slap-bang-whoosh* all over the lino."

"Super sorrow! I'll pick it up later. Can't stop now—*Operation Rush-hour,*" Venables called over his shoulder as he disappeared round the corner.

"What cheek! Wait till I catch him!" Jennings muttered to himself, stooping to retrieve the bottle.

As he did so, a headlong rush of boys came charging hot-foot along the corridor on their way to the notice-board . . . Too late, they saw the danger ahead. Before they could stop, the leader of the hot-footed chargers had skidded on to the slippery oil-bath where he floundered crazily like a clown in an ice-pantomime. Then his feet shot from under him and he sat down heavily, tripping up the rest of the party pressing hard on him from behind.

In a moment, the corridor was a heaving mass of waving arms and kicking legs . . . and it was this scene of chaos and turmoil that greeted Mr. Wilkins as he came striding along the landing on a tour of duty.

"What on earth are you boys playing at?" he demanded, as the victims sorted themselves out and rose unsteadily to their feet.

"Please, sir, we had a crash," volunteered Atkinson. "I think somebody's been polishing the lino, sir."

"It's only bat-oil," Jennings explained. "I was just oiling my bat, you see, sir."

"Oh, were you! Well, you'd no business to be doing it

53

The corridor was a mass of waving arms and legs

indoors," retorted Mr. Wilkins. "The pavilion is the proper place for cricket gear; and if I see you playing around with that bat again inside the building, I shall confiscate it. Now, wipe up that oil—at once."

"Yes, sir."

The boy bent to his task, and Mr. Wilkins uttered an exasperated cry of protest. "No, no, no: not with your handkerchief, you silly little boy! Use a rag. Where's the rag you were oiling the bat with?"

Jennings swallowed hard and crossed his fingers: "That *was* my handkerchief I was using, sir!"

"*Doh!* Go and fetch a mop from the kitchen and do the job properly," Mr. Wilkins ordered: and, turning to the interested spectators, he added: "Don't stand there blocking the corridor, you boys. It's bad enough having the place turned ankle-deep into a slough of despond, without people paddling about and treading it all over the lino."

Clutching his bat in one hand and his empty bottle in the other, Jennings trotted downstairs behind the unwilling skaters.

In the hall he stopped to read the notice on the board, and at once he was filled with a joy and elation that swept all thoughts of mopping-up operations from his mind.

"*At the invitation of Lieut.-General Sir Melville Merridew, D.S.O., M.C., the first and second cricket elevens will attend the Dunhambury County Ground on Thursday,*" the notice read. "*The remainder of the school will go for a picnic.*"

Jennings crowed with joy. So they were going to be taken to a county match! And the second eleven, too! That meant that he would be going, and Venables and Temple and Bromwich; most of his friends, in fact . . . But not Darbishire!

Never in the history of cricket, Jennings maintained, had there been such a butter-fingered bungler as C. E. J. Darbishire. True, he was desperately keen to improve his performance, but for all his efforts he remained as clumsy on a cricket pitch as an elk on an escalator.

It was disappointing, because he had made a profound study of the game. He could recite, by heart, the batting and bowling averages of the foremost county players; and, when safely away from the cricket field, he would demonstrate to boys smaller than himself the proper way to play a forward stroke or bowl a leg-spinner. It was only when he came face to face with reality in the shape of a hard leather ball that his theories failed to stand the test, and he found himself quite unable to hit, stop, catch, throw or even *see* the wretched thing until it was too late. However, no one could deny his prowess as a scorer, and it was in this capacity that he faithfully served the Linbury second eleven.

If only the General's invitation could be extended to include scorers! It would be a thousand times better if Darbishire could come with them, Jennings reasoned, instead of having to go for the picnic which was scheduled for the rest of the school . . . He hurried off to the staff room to plead the cause of his friend.

"Sir, please, sir, is there any chance of scorers coming too?" he asked Mr. Carter, whom he found marking books at the staff room table. "You see, Darbishire's terribly keen, sir, but his cricket is so feeble that he knows he'll never get in the team, and—well, it makes him go broody, sir."

"Broody!" Mr. Carter raised a puzzled eyebrow. "You mean it makes him brood?"

"Well, both really, sir. He knows he plays like an old hen and he worries about it. So if he *could* come, sir . . .!"

Mr. Carter considered. The headmaster would surely raise no objection. After all, it was largely due to Jennings and Darbishire that the General had suggested this treat in the first place. In fact, the Old Boy would probably feel most indignant if he thought that one of his young friends was not going to be amongst those present.

"Very well, then, Jennings," Mr. Carter said at length. "First and second eleven scorers may come as well."

"Oh, thank you, sir. Darbishire will be as pleased as a guinea-pig with one tail."

56

Jennings scuttled happily from the room, intent on finding Darbishire and breaking the good news without delay. He still clutched his cricket-bat, although by this time he had completely forgotten his unfinished task in the corridor.

But Mr. Wilkins hadn't forgotten! Even as Jennings was scampering round in seach of his friend, so he, in his turn, was being sought by Mr. Wilkins.

The duty master's expression was stern and forbidding as he strode from room to room. Far from being in a mood to pour oil on troubled waters, he was extremely angry to find that Jennings had not already applied some water to the troublesome oil.

Darbishire was designing a new type of flying-saucer on the cover of his history book, when Jennings burst into Classroom 3 waving his cricket bat round his head like a battle-axe.

"I say, Darbi—what d'you think! I'll give you three guesses," he cried eagerly.

"Whatever I guess it's bound to be wrong—it always is," Darbishire observed, scarcely glancing up from his blue-print.

"I'll tell you, then: you remember that old geezer that we made a bit of a bish over, and locked in the library by mistake?"

Darbishire nodded. The incident was still fresh in his memory.

"Well, we're getting that holiday he woffled about, and what's more he's very decently treating the first and second elevens to a day at the county cricket ground next Thursday."

"Gosh! You lucky bazookas. I wish *I* was in the team."

"That's what I was going to tell you. Mr. Carter says scorers can count."

Darbishire looked up from his drawing. "Of course they can count," he retorted. "They wouldn't be much use for adding up the scores if they couldn't."

"No, you clodpoll! He means they count as being in

57

the team. In other words, you're coming to Dunhambury with us."

"What? Golly, how super-wacko-sonic!" The scorer's eyes shone behind his dusty spectacles. He leaped to his feet and waggled his head from side to side in joyful glee. "I'm jolly well going to take my autograph book with me and see how many signatures I can get. I've got six pink pages left specially blank for famous sporting characters."

"Good scheme! Try and get R. J. Findlater's autograph, if he's playing," Jennings advised. "I saw him play against the Australians last year. You should just see his super-sonic off-drives!" He smote the air with his bat in eager demonstration. Then he said: "Give me a bowl with the black-board duster, and I'll show you how he zonks a boundary over the bowler's head."

"We can't play cricket in the classroom," Darbishire demurred.

"Just one bowl—that's all. Screw the duster up into a ball, so you'll be able to chuck it."

Gingerly, Darbishire picked up the black-board duster, a shower of chalk dust powdering his shoes as he rolled it into a roughly spherical shape.

"Phew! It's terribly chalky. Shouldn't think it's been shaken out since the Stone Age," he observed. Then he tossed the improvised ball to Jennings, who jumped forward and smote it with all the force at his command.

It was unfortunate that Mr. Wilkins should choose that precise moment to enter the room . . . For as he opened the door, the misguided missile struck the lintel above his head, dropped neatly on to his right shoulder, and left him choking and gasping in a blinding blizzard of chalk dust, as thick as a snow storm on the South Col of Mount Everest.

For some moments Jennings and Darbishire stared at the blizzard-bound master in speechless dismay. Mr. Wilkins, also, remained silent, but only because his nose and throat were so full of chalk dust that speech was out of the question. At last he found his voice.

"Jennings! . . . Darbishire! What's the meaning of this?"

"Terribly sorry, sir," Jennings mumbled. "I—er—I didn't know you were coming in just then, sir."

He hurried forward to brush the avalanche from the master's shoulders, but the offer of help was curtly rejected.

"I've had just about enough of your nonsense for one day," said Mr. Wilkins, bristling dangerously. "I came in here to find you because you've left the corridor swimming ankle-deep in bat-oil; and now, as soon as I open the door you start bombarding me with chalky dusters full of dusty chalk dust." He glared at the boys through the powdery pall and held out his hand for the bat. "Give that to me, Jennings. I warned you that I should confiscate it if I found you using it indoors. And as a further punishment for this outrageous behaviour, you can both stay in on Thursday and work through some exercises in your English Grammar books."

The room swam before Jennings' eyes, and a cold, empty feeling gripped him in the pit of the stomach.

"Thursday, sir?" he quavered. "Oh, please sir, not Thursday. We're going to Dunhambury to watch the county cricket, sir."

"You mean you *were* going to Dunhambury," Mr. Wilkins corrected. "But that was before you chose to play indoor cricket instead. You can both report to me after breakfast on Thursday morning, and I'll set you some work to keep you busy till lunch time."

This was tragedy . . . This was the end of everything! Mr. Wilkins could not possibly have devised a more heart-breaking punishment. And what made it even worse, Jennings thought bitterly, was that he had only just obtained permission for Darbishire to join the party!

What a waste of permission that had been! What a hollow mockery of his well-meaning efforts! Besides, he reasoned, it was most unfair that Darbishire should have to share in the punishment when he hadn't done anything to deserve it—well, *hardly* anything. He put this point to Mr. Wilkins.

"It was all my fault, really, sir, so please need Darbishire stay behind too, sir?"

"Of course he stays behind," the master retorted. "He should have thought of the consequences before he joined you in this—this wave of juvenile delinquency, and took to playing test matches all over the classroom."

He paused, and suddenly felt uncomfortable at the sight of the distressed and woebegone figures standing miserably before him. He had meant to punish them severely, but all the same it came as something of a shock to him to see their faces so racked with anguish and haggard with grief.

It has been said that Mr. Wilkins suffered from a kind heart. He was aware of this, and did his utmost to ignore its promptings when it suggested—as it did then—that he should mix a little mercy with the dose of justice which he was in the act of dispensing. "Let them off more lightly: give them some other form of punishment," urged the Kind Heart, while the sterner side of his character counselled: "Stand no nonsense. Be firm: don't let them get away with it."

Mr. Wilkins considered the advice from both sides of his nature, and decided to take a middle course. He would say nothing about letting them off part of their punishment, but would set them to work, as arranged, and keep them at it until their colleagues were lining up on the quad, ready to march off to the bus stop.

Then, at the very last moment, when all hope of reprieve had faded, he would appear like some fairy godmother to rescue them from their misery and send them off rejoicing to join their fellows.

That, at any rate, was Mr. Wilkins' intention. It was sheer mischance that his plan did not work out as he had hoped.

For the time being, however, he decided to give them no hint that a reprieve was likely, or even possible. He stood frowning with disapproval as Darbishire blew his nose to conceal his grief, and Jennings tottered out of the room in a daze of despair, to continue his mopping-up operations in the corridor.

CHAPTER 7

DISTINGUISHED COMPANY

ON THURSDAY morning, Jennings and Darbishire sat poring over their grammar books, while their more fortunate colleagues lined up in the dining hall for the packets of sandwiches which Matron had prepared for their lunch.

After breakfast, Jennings had made a last despairing appeal to Mr. Wilkins' better nature. "Sir, *please*, sir, if we get the work done before the bus goes, may we go too, please, sir?"

"Time to talk about that when you've finished it," Mr. Wilkins had answered; and had then set them enough work to keep them occupied until the Dunhambury party would have left the premises.

"It's a mouldy chizz," Jennings grumbled as he settled down in the classroom. "If Old Wilkie'd got any decency he'd let us off."

"He said we could go when we've finished," Darbishire reminded him, scribbling away at top speed. "If only I could write with both hands and one foot at the same time, I might just about be able to do it."

Jennings shook his head. "A fat lot of good that would do you! He wants to see the work when we've done it, don't forget. That means *he's* not going to the match, and he's going to take jolly good care that *we* don't go, either."

An hour later, the sound of footsteps scrunching on the gravel outside announced that the teams were lining up for their departure. Picnic lunches bulged from the raincoat pockets of everyone—except Bromwich who had eaten his already, and was wondering how he was going to survive the long hours of famine that lay ahead.

Jennings put down his pen and went over to the window to watch them go. He saw Mr. Carter calling the roll and forming the straggling knots of boys into a shapely crocodile: he heard him give the order to start off down the drive . . . And then he saw Mr. Wilkins hurry out on to the quad and join his colleague at the end of the file.

So Mr. Wilkins was going too! . . . Jennings blinked in surprise. How, then, could they show him their work when they had finished it? And what a rotter the man must be, Jennings reflected, that he could calmly waltz off to watch county matches, leaving poor unfortunate wretches cooped up in a classroom.

It must be said in Mr. Wilkins' favour that he really had no intention of acting in such a hard-hearted manner. When the arrangements for the holiday had been announced, it was decided that the headmaster and Mr. Carter should go to Dunhambury, while the picnic should be surpervised by Mr. Wilkins and Mr. Hind, a tall thin young man who taught art and music throughout the school.

Then, at the last moment, Mr. Pemberton-Oakes had been obliged to stay behind, and had sent a message asking Mr. Wilkins to go in his place.

Mr. Wilkins was delighted, for he had not been looking forward to the picnic with much enthusiasm: and in the rush and scurry of last-minute preparations he completely forgot to release Jennings and Darbishire from their punishment.

He remembered it forty minutes later as he was alighting from the bus near the Dunhambury cricket ground. Immediately a qualm of conscience attacked him.

"Oh, my goodness! Why on earth didn't I think of them before?" he reproached himself. But by then it was too late to do anything about it. He soothed his conscience with the thought that they would still be able to go for the picnic with Mr. Hind. Perhaps they would enjoy that just as much . . . *Perhaps!*

Jennings remained watching at the window until the cricket teams disappeared round the bend of the drive. Then he returned to his desk, jaded in spirit.

"Old Wilkie's gone too," he announced bitterly. "Doesn't that just prove how unfair grown-ups are? They sentence you to ghastly punishments, and then stonk off to enjoy themselves with a light laugh. Tt! You can get away with anything when you're grown up!"

They worked in silence for a further half-hour. Then Darbishire threw down his pen and said: "Phew! That's the last exercise finished, thank goodness!" . . . And a few minutes later Jennings blotted his work with his handkerchief and closed his book.

"I say, Darbi, I've just thought of something," he exclaimed. "Old Wilkie wants to see this work as soon as it's finished. He said so, after breakfast."

"He's going to be unlucky, then. We can't show it to him if he isn't here, can we?"

Jennings leaped to his feet, his eyes shining with inspiration. "Yes, but don't you see? That gives us a jolly good excuse to dash off to Dunhambury after him! After all, he didn't say we *weren't* to go, and we can't show him the stuff unless we *do*."

Darbishire was thunderstruck by this brilliant reasoning. "But what will he say when he sees us?" he gasped.

"He ought to be jolly pleased. If he's as keen on correcting these exercises as he makes out, he can sit and read them all afternoon."

Darbishire blinked nervously through his spectacles. Much as he would have liked to watch the match, he viewed Jennings' plan with misgiving. He sought in his mind for some objection.

"Yes, but how can we get there? It's at least five miles to Dunhambury," he said.

"We'll go by bus. I've got two shillings, so that'll just do it."

"Yes, but if we spend that on bus fares we shan't have any entrance money left to get into the ground with," Darbishire pointed out. "Mr. Carter's paying for all the other chaps, don't forget. We shall have to fork up out of our own pockets."

Jennings had not thought of that. It was unthinkable that his brilliant scheme should fail for lack of financial support.

"Well, you think of something then, instead of just sitting there like a stick of rhubarb, picking holes in everything I suggest," he said heatedly. "I've thought up the sizzling brainwave: the least you can do is to work out the details."

There was silence for some moments while they racked their brains for some way out of the difficulty. Then Darbishire said thoughtfully: "If only we could borrow a couple of bikes from the day boys, we'd get there in no time, and still have enough cash to get into the ground. You see, we could take that short cut through Farmer Arrowsmith's meadow, and avoid the long stretch through Linbury village."

"Yes, that'd save quite a bit of time," Jennings agreed eagerly. "And when we got to the ground we could leave the bikes in the car park and join the other chaps in time for lunch . . . Let's do that, shall we?"

"We can't. The day boys aren't here this morning, so there aren't any bikes to borrow."

Jennings "tut-tutted" in annoyance. "Well, why suggest going on bikes, if you knew it was out of the question?"

"I was just thinking what a decent scheme it *would* have been if we *could* have," Darbishire explained. "My father says we should always look on the bright side of . . ."

Jennings was in no mood to listen to the wise sayings of the Reverend Percival Darbishire. He turned away with an impatient gesture and paced up and down the room seeking an answer to the transport problem. Suddenly he stopped in mid-stride and said: "I know! We'll hitch-hike! Someone's bound to give us a lift if we flap our fingers at all the cars that come along, and then we'll still have my two shillings for when we get there."

Darbishire still looked doubtful, but his objections were

over-ruled. Here was his chance, Jennings pointed out, to fill the blank pink pages of his album with the autographs of famous sporting celebrities. Why, it was more than likely that R. J. Findlater, the *England* amateur, would be playing for the county side. It would be monstrous to let slip such a golden opportunity for securing the great man's autograph . . . Very well, then, what were they waiting for?

There was no time to lose, for the precious minutes of the morning were slipping away. Jennings folded the exercise books in half, and stuffed them into his pocket, while Darbishire took the treasured album from his desk.

Then, they hastened downstairs and out on to the quad. Away to their right they could see Mr. Hind and his party of juniors setting off across the cricket field to enjoy a picnic on the Downs.

"There's no one about—let's get moving," Jennings said, and led the way down the drive and out on to the Dunhambury road.

For some while their efforts to obtain a lift met with no success. Car after car swept past at top speed, heedless of the hopping figures waving exercise books wildly from the side of the road.

As they climbed the hill towards Linbury village, Darbishire said: "I'm getting fed up with this. I've pretty well jerked both thumbs out of their sockets and flapped my hand off at the wrist, and nothing has even *looked* like stopping, except that chap on a bike who was going the wrong way."

"He only stopped because you nearly conked him on the head with your autograph album," Jennings pointed out. "You don't have to wave the thing round like a helicopter, you know."

He looked back along the way they had come, and saw a green sports car racing up the hill towards them. It did not look the kind of vehicle that would stop in response to their signals, but Jennings waved at it all the same.

The car shot past them, gained the crest of the hill and

65

then stopped. A man with a large ginger moustache poked his head out of the driving window and beckoned to them.

"Wow! Petrified paintpots! He's stopped for us," cried Jennings in delight. They charged up the hill in the wake of the car, and arrived panting and breathless at the top.

"I say, excuse me, but could you very kindly give us a lift, please?" Jennings gasped.

The man opened the near-side door, and Jennings stepped back politely to allow his wheezing colleague to enter first.

"After you, Darbishire," he said.

"No, after you, Jennings."

"No, no: you first."

"Make up your minds—I'm in a hurry," the driver remarked briskly: whereupon the two boys scrambled in together and sat on the edge of the back seat, breathing heavily.

"This is very kind of you," panted Darbishire. "The other chaps all went by bus, but we had to stay behind and do our exercises."

"Splendid! Nothing like plenty of exercise to keep you fit," said the man with the ginger moustache as he let in the clutch.

"Not *those* sort of exercises. Ours were the other sort, with subjects, verbs and objects and things," Jennings explained. "Anyway, we're trying to get to Dunhambury to watch the cricket. You don't happen to be going anywhere near the county ground by any chance, do you?"

"Your luck's in. That's just where I am going," the driver replied.

Jennings smiled his gratitude and settled himself more comfortably in the back seat. Some bulky object was obstructing his feet, and glancing down he saw a large leather cricket bag lying on the floor.

A cricket bag! And the man was going to the county ground! . . . Jennings shot a quick look at the driver, but his features were not visible from the back seat. With

66

mounting excitement he asked: "Excuse me, but you aren't *playing* in the match, are you?"

The man nodded. "That's why I'm in a hurry to get there. I had a spot of engine trouble a few miles back, or I should have been there long ago."

He shifted slightly in his seat, and as he did so his features were reflected in the driving mirror above the windscreen. "Fortunately we're batting this morning, so I dare say they'll be able to get along without me until lunch time."

Jennings scarcely heard the last remark, for he was staring intently at the reflection in the driving mirror. Why, of course! Now that he could see the man's face, there was no longer any doubt about his identity. And the ginger moustache proved it! . . . For photographs of R. J. Findlater, *Sussex* and *England*, had appeared so often in newspapers and on television that he was easily recognised by any follower of first-class cricket.

After the first shock of joyful surprise, Jennings took his courage in both hands and said: "Excuse me, sir, but I think I've seen you before. You *are* Mr. R. J. Findlater, aren't you?"

The cricketer admitted his identity. "Quite correct . . . And you?"

"I'm Jennings and this is Darbishire. We're both very keen cricketers, too, of course, but I don't suppose you've ever heard of us, though. I'm in the Linbury Court second eleven and Darbishire's our scorer."

It seemed that their fame in the world of cricket had not reached Mr. Findlater's ears, but he nodded and said: "Oh, yes," to show that he was interested.

Darbishire sat listening to the snatches of conversation, spell-bound with wonder . . . So this was the one-and-only R. J. Findlater—in person! And he, C. E. J. Darbishire, was actually sitting less than three feet away from the great man—so close that he could have leaned forward and touched him, if such an action would not have led to embarrassing explanations.

He felt pleased and proud, yet so absurdly shy that he

67

could do nothing but wriggle his fingers and toes and goggle at the England all-rounder, as though he were some superhuman specimen that the dauntless Butch Breakaway had discovered on the moon.

Jennings nudged his friend in the ribs, and whispered: "Well, go on, Darbi, say something. Don't just sit there and gape like a stuffed mattress, with your eyes popping out like organ stops. Haven't you ever met any famous sporting characters before?"

Darbishire pulled himself together with an effort.

"Oh yes, of course. I was—er—I was just thinking what a funny thing it was that Mr. Findlater should give us a lift; because it was all through him that we couldn't go with the others."

The cricketer raised a ginger eyebrow. "All though me? And what did I do, pray?"

"Oh, it wasn't really your fault—you needn't blame yourself," Jennings hastened to assure him. "I was just demonstrating to Darbishire how you do those supersonic clouts to leg, with a chalky duster, and one of our masters came in and caught it *slap-bang-wallop* in the target area."

Mr. Findlater's hearty laugh put them at their ease, and from then onwards they felt quite at home in his distinguished presence.

They talked about cricket. Jennings picked up some useful hints on how to bowl leg-spinners: Darbishire quoted Mr. Findlater's latest batting average more accurately than the cricketer could have done himself; and then went on to announce that the figure was exactly ten times greater than Jennings' second eleven average of 5.83 recurring.

They were approaching the Dunhambury cricket ground when Darbishire produced his album from his pocket, and said: "I say, Mr. Findlater, will you ever so kindly sign my autograph book for me, please? I've got six pink pages left blank specially for sporting characters."

"I can't write while I'm driving: let me have the book, and I'll do it later on."

"Coo, thanks!" Darbishire slipped the album into the leather cricket bag to ensure that it would be to hand when a more suitable moment arrived.

Already in his mind's eye he could picture the sensation that the autograph would cause amongst his friends in Form 3. Upon his return to school, he would leave the book lying open, as though by chance; and when some-one drew attention to the great man's signature, he would say airily: "Yes, I thought I'd get Findlater to dash off something for my album" . . . There would be a buzz of admiration, after which he could hear himself saying: "Of course, you couldn't expect an important chap like Find-later to sign just *anybody's* book. He did it for me as a special favour from one cricket enthusiast to another."

As he fastened the bag he prattled hopefully: "And perhaps you'd even ask some of the other players to sign their names, too. Only, tell them to keep to the pink pages or they'll get mixed up with the television stars and all that crush. Just their names and initials will be enough; but if they really want to write a bit more, like, say for instance, 'By hook or by crook I'll be last in your book,' all they've got to do is to rub out Jennings' scribble on the last page and . . . "

At that moment the car turned in through the gates of the county ground, and came to rest in the players' car park. Jennings pointed out that they had not paid for admission, but Mr. Findlater waved aside the proffered shillings and invited them into the Members' Enclosure as his guests. Then he hurried into the pavilion to change, leaving the boys thrilling with excitement.

The Members' Enclosure! . . . Comfortable deck chairs . . . Padded seats . . . And the Linbury Court party on the far side of the ground were having to make do with hard wooden benches!

Some time—but not *too* soon—they would have to seek out Mr. Wilkins and report to him. But first of all they would enjoy their few minutes of glory, sitting importantly in the Members' Enclosure as guests of one of England's foremost players.

They sank into their deck chairs with sighs of pure happiness. This was the life!

CHAPTER 8

AUTOGRAPH FOR DARBISHIRE

SUSSEX HAD been batting all morning against a strong M.C.C. side, and shortly before the luncheon interval the scoreboard showed that they were approaching the "hundred up" for the loss of four wickets.

On the far side of the ground, Mr. Carter and Mr. Wilkins sat watching the game with the group of Linbury boys lying on raincoats at their feet.

Temple had borrowed Mr. Carter's binoculars and was sweeping the field with his gaze, pausing every now and then to give a running commentary to his fellows on little details of the play which could not be seen with the naked eye.

"That chap fielding at cover point has just broken his boot-lace," he announced. "The square leg umpire's got a moustache and four sweaters . . . I can see the wicket keeper scratching his ear ever so plainly . . ."

"Let me have a look," begged Venables.

"Wait a sec; I haven't finished yet." His gaze roamed farther, swept past the scoring-box and came to rest on the pavilion. "I can see a seagull on the roof," he exclaimed. "And down below, at grown level, I can see . . . Gosh! Wow! . . . Fossilised fish-hooks!"

"What's up?" queried Atkinson.

"I can see Jennings and Darbishire in the Members' Enclosure!"

Mr. Wilkins gave a little start. He still had an uneasy feeling of guilt for having left the boys behind, and at the mention of their names he turned upon Temple in some annoyance.

"Don't talk such ridiculous nonsense, you silly little boy. If that's all you want the binoculars for, pass them on to someone who can talk sense."

"But I *can* see them, honestly, sir," Temple protested.

"You're imagining things. Must be looking through the wrong end of the glasses, or something."

All the same, Mr. Wilkins focused his own field-glasses upon the place in question. Immediately his jaw dropped, and he opened his eyes wide in surprise.

"Good heavens! I say, Carter, the boy's right. It *is* Jennings and Darbishire. How on earth did they get here? I left them doing an English exercise—picking out objects and things."

Mr. Carter retrieved his binoculars. "*You* seem to have picked out some objects, too, Wilkins," he observed. "Yes, I can see them quite plainly through the glasses. You'd better go and investigate at once before the lunch interval."

Mr. Wilkins was already on his feet. "I certainly will. I'm going straight over this minute."

"Oh, but sir, you can't, sir," cried Temple.

"Oh! And why not?"

"Because they're in the private enclosure, sir. They won't let ordinary people like you in, unless you're a member, sir."

"I—I—Corwumph!" said Mr. Wilkins, and hurried off to follow the boundary circuit to the far side of the ground.

Jennings and Darbishire saw him coming when he was still some distance away. At once their feeling of glorious importance faded, leaving a cold emptiness in its place.

Back at school, Jennings had felt confident about the ready answer he had prepared for Mr. Wilkins. Now, he was not so sure. The reasons which had seemed so convincing in the classroom might sound hollow, now that the moment had come to recite them in cold blood. He swallowed hard and crossed his fingers. Then, followed by Darbishire, he rose to his feet and walked with faltering steps down to the enclosure rails.

"Jennings! Darbishire! What are you doing in there?"

cried Mr. Wilkins. In his state of agitation he seemed more concerned at the thought of the boys committing a trespass, than the fact that they had no business to be in Dunhambury at all. "Don't you know you're not allowed inside those railings—it's reserved for members only!"

"Yes, I know, sir; we came in as guests. Mr. R. J. Findlater gave us permission, sir."

Mr. Wilkins stared unbelievingly. "Nonsense! You don't expect me to believe that, do you?"

"Honestly, sir. We sort of met him by chance, you see. And then I happened to mention that I played cricket for the second eleven, and as one cricketer to another he brought us along, sir," Jennings explained.

"Oh, did he!" retorted Mr. Wilkins, as the boys came out through the little gate, and stood before him. "And did you also happen to mention, as one cricketer to another, that you were supposed to be at school doing some work for me?"

The moment had arrived for the explanation.

"Well, that was really why we came as a matter of fact, sir," Jennings replied in what he hoped was a casual tone. "You said we'd got to bring you the work as soon as we'd done it, and—er, well, we didn't want to disappoint you, sir."

When spoken aloud, Jennings thought it sounded the flimsiest excuse that he had ever been called upon to make. He braced himself to withstand the onslaught of Mr. Wilkins' anger, which he felt certain would follow.

It never came!

For the first time since he had arrived at Dunhambury, Mr. Wilkins' conscience had ceased to trouble him. After all, he had meant the boys to come . . . And come they certainly had! There was little point, therefore, in assuming an indignation which he did not feel.

"You needn't have bothered about bringing the punishment along—that would have kept until later," he replied, in so friendly a tone that the boys gaped at him in astonishment. "Now, you'd better come and join the rest of the party."

"Yes, sir . . . Thank you, sir."

They followed him, marvelling at this change of mood, for which they could find no reason. But then, grown-ups were like that: there was just no accounting for the way they looked at things!

They arrived at the far side of the ground as the teams were going into the pavilion for lunch. As he sat down on the hard wooden bench, Mr. Wilkins said: "Come along, Jennings and Darbishire. You'd better share my sandwiches, seeing that you've come without anything to eat."

It was a perfect day for cricket. Mr. Findlater was at the top of his form; and after the luncheon interval he went in to bat, and delighted the crowd with a brilliant innings which reached treble figures before he was caught at the wicket.

All afternoon long, Jennings and Darbishire sat on the grass discussing each scoring stroke and absorbing every dctail of the play. This, they decided, was a holiday they would never forget.

As it happened they were right, though it was not until it was time for them to leave that the afternoon was made memorable in a way that neither of them could foresee.

"Come along, you boys: it's time we were going," Mr. Carter said, shortly before the end of play.

They lined up in a straggling crocodile and moved off towards the main gate. But they had not gone far when Darbishire uttered a sudden wail of dismay.

"Fossilised fish-hooks! My autograph album—I'd forgotten all about it!"

He darted out of the line and ran back to report his loss to the two masters who were bringing up the rear.

"Sir, sir! I can't go yet, sir: I've got to get my album first, sir!"

"Too late now, boy. You'll have to go without it," said Mr. Wilkins.

Darbishire hopped up and down in agitation.

"Oh, but sir, I can't sir! It's frightfully invaluable, sir. It's got all sorts of people in it—sporting characters, television stars, famous authors and our window-cleaner's brother who won a football pool, sir."

Mr. Carter glanced at his watch. "Hurry up then, Darbishire. Get the book and come straight out and join us by the main gate."

"May I go with him, sir?" Jennings asked, appearing suddenly at his friend's side. "He may need someone to help him find it, sir."

"Quickly, then, Jennings. There's no time to lose if we're going to catch the six-thirty bus."

The two boys raced off towards the pavilion at top speed: but when they arrived at the entrance their way was barred by an official-looking gentleman in a shiny peaked cap, holding a stack of score-cards in his hand. He looked at them without enthusiasm.

"Good-afternoon: is Mr. R. J. Findlater in, please?" Darbishire inquired politely.

"Not now, he isn't. He went in fifth wicket down, just after lunch," the man replied.

"No, I don't mean is he still batting. I mean, is he at home to callers, as you might say? You see, he's got my autograph book and I want to ask him for it back."

The attendant showed no eagerness to help. It was his duty to keep unauthorised persons out of the pavilion, and he was not going to be tricked by any crafty autograph hunter trying on some dodge to get past him.

"Well, you can't go in, and that's that! You'll have to wait till he comes out," he answered.

"Oh, fish-hooks! This is frantic," groaned Darbishire. "Well, look here, if I wait outside will you very decently go in and find him for me?"

The seller of score-cards shook his head. "Can't leave the gate. Besides, it doesn't do to go disturbing people while they're watching a last-wicket stand."

Darbishire danced with frustration and despair. "But it's urgent: I've got to catch a bus!"

The unhelpful one shrugged and turned away.

"It's no good hanging about here. I vote we nip round to the back of the pav," Jennings suggested. "We might

74

be able to see Mr. Findlater and wave to him through the window."

They scurried round to the rear of the building where a row of windows overlooked a deserted part of the cricket ground. One of the windows was open, and the boys stood on tip-toe and peered through into what was obviously a changing-room. Jackets hung on pegs round the walls, cricket gear lay upon the floor, and in the middle of the room was a table on which stood a large leather bag, with the initials "R.J.F." stamped on the side.

"Look, there's his bag. I bet my book's in it," cried Darbishire excitedly. "If only we could get it!"

"Why not! I'll give you a leg-up through the window," Jennings suggested.

Darbishire hesitated. "Oh golly, no! I can't just barge in without permission. I might get arrested or something."

"Don't be so stark raving feeble, Darbi. You can't be arrested for claiming your own property; you've got a perfect right to go in and take it."

Darbishire pondered the matter for a moment, and then made up his mind. "Well, all right, then; but you've jolly well got to come in with me."

"Of course, I will," Jennings agreed. "After all, it's the only way to get your book back, isn't it?"

With some difficulty the boys clambered over the sill. Once inside the room they had no intention of loitering. Darbishire made a dive for the cricket bag. Sure enough, his album was tucked inside where he had left it. He seized the book and darted back to the window.

Jennings turned to follow: and as he did so he was suddenly aware that they were not alone. He glanced down the length of the room . . .

At the far end, near the door, almost hidden by a tall clothes rack, a short, thin man in a shabby blue suit was standing quite still, and eyeing their movements with suspicious interest.

So they *had* been seen climbing through the window!

Jennings went hot and cold with embarrassment. Whatever must the little man be thinking? . . . He must be told the true facts at once!

Jennings hurried down the changing-room, apologising as he went.

"I say, I'm sorry we came beetling in like that, but it's perfectly all right, really," he explained. He waved his arm vaguely in the direction of Darbishire. "You see, this chap wanted his autograph book, because we've got to catch a bus."

The little man gave him a shifty look, and said nothing. It was clear that the visitors were not welcome.

Jennings had an odd feeling that all was not well. He looked hard at the shabby little man, trying to recall whether he had seen him at the wicket earlier in the afternoon. Obviously, Jennings reasoned, he must be a member of the batting side who had finished his innings, or he would not already have changed back into his seedy serge suit. Yet he didn't look like a cricketer! Perhaps he was a groundsman, or some friend of one of the players? Whoever he was, he seemed to resent the boy's presence very strongly.

Darbishire was half-way through the window before he realised what was happening. Immediately, he came hurrying back to join his friend, holding the treasured album aloft.

"We couldn't get permission to come in the front way," he pointed out. "But this is my book, right enough. I can show you my name inside to prove it, if you don't believe me." A bright idea occurred to him, and he added: "I say, would you very decently sign it for me, please?"

The shabby man looked surprised.

"I mean, you *are* one of the county players, aren't you?" Darbishire gave a little nervous laugh and went on: "Yes, of course you must be, or you wouldn't be in the changing-room, would you?"

By this time the little man had sized up the situation. He had good reasons for not wishing to sign his name or announce his business. On the other hand, he reckoned that the quickest way to get rid of an autograph hunter was to accede to his request.

He took the book from Darbishire's outstretched hand, and fumbled in his pocket for a pencil. Then he paused for a moment in thought, as though uncertain what to write. Finally he scribbled something on the proffered pink page, and gave the book back to its grateful owner.

"Got to be off now: train to catch," he muttered, sidling furtively towards the door . . . The next moment he was gone.

"Well, that was a bit of luck. Fancy bagging another county cricketer as easily as that. I wonder who he . . ."

Darbishire broke off and stared at the autograph in bewilderment. "Hey, just a mo: something's gone haywire! Look what he's written in my book . . . *R. J. Findlater*!"

Jennings glanced down at the signature and a look of puzzled wonder spread over his features.

"But that's crazy! That chap wasn't Findlater—that's about the one person we *do* know he wasn't; so why should ! 2 pretend he is?"

"I don't know: perhaps he's a forger," Darbishire hazarded.

"Don't be a clodpoll! What's the point of forging an autograph book?"

"Must have been a feeble sort of joke, then," Darbishire decided, annoyed that his precious pink pages had been sullied in this way.

"Never mind; you've got your book back—that's the main thing," Jennings consoled him. "We'd better get cracking now. Old Wilkie will go berserk if we keep him waiting much longer."

He turned back towards the window; but before he had time to climb over the sill, the door opened and a tall figure wearing a ginger moustache and white flannels appeared on the threshold.

"Goodness! Here *is* Mr. Findlater!" Jennings exclaimed. "I say, congratulations on your century, sir."

The cricketer had not expected to find the room occupied.

"Thank you," he replied. "But what are you two boys doing in here? You've no business to be in the changing-room, you know."

"I know, sir. We just came in for my album," Darbishire explained.

"Oh, yes, of course. I'm afraid I haven't written anything in it yet. I'll do it for you now."

Darbishire shook his head sorrowfully. "It's too late. It's been done already by somebody else!"

"Eh? I don't understand!"

So they told him about the little man in the shabby blue suit and showed him the mysterious forgery.

Mr. Findlater smiled when he saw the bogus signature. "Someone's been pulling your leg," he told them. "Wait while I get my fountain pen, and I'll give you the genuine article."

He unhooked his jacket from a peg, and felt in the inside pocket. Then, distinctly puzzled, he rummaged in his other pockets . . . All to no purpose: for not only his fountain pen, but also his wallet, his watch, his loose change—every article of value—had disappeared from the brown tweed suit hanging on his peg.

"Do you boys know anything about this?" he asked, turning to them with a worried frown. "Someone's walked off with all my possessions!"

"What!"

They stared at him; first in bewilderment and then with dawning horror in case he should think that they might have had something to do with it. After all, he had discovered them trespassing on private premises: he had almost caught them in the act of climbing out again through the window. Such behaviour was enough to arouse anyone's suspicions.

"You—you don't think it was us, surely!" gasped Jennings.

"I don't know what to think," returned Mr. Findlater, running his hands over his team-mates' jacket and trousers hanging on the adjoining pegs. "All I know is, the whole

78

team appears to have been robbed of everything they left in their pockets."

The answer came to Jennings in a flash.

"I've got it!" he cried excitedly. "The chap who signed Darbishire's book! That's why he pretended to be one of the players when we found him in the changing-room!"

"Gosh, yes!" Darbishire broke in. "And when we asked him for his signature, I suppose he just scribbled down the first cricketer's name he could think of."

"Was he carrying a bag or anything, did you notice?" Mr. Findlater asked.

"No, he wasn't; but his pockets looked jolly bulgy."

"Come along, then: let's see if we can find him. He can't be far away."

Mr. Findlater wasted no time. He dashed out of the changing-room up to the main lobby, and then down the broad flight of steps past the members' enclosure, and out on to the cricket ground . . . Behind him ran Jennings and Darbishire, flushed with excitement and proud to be helping the great man in his hour of need.

The umpire had just called "Last Over" when they emerged from the pavilion, and already many people were making their way towards the exit. Mr. Findlater stopped short, a few yards from the main gate. "Are you sure you'll know this chap again?" he asked.

"Oh, yes, easily, sir. We couldn't mistake him," Jennings answered, straining his eyes at the crowd in the hope of seeing their quarry.

Darbishire, also, cast an eye over the milling throng; but his other eye was keeping a look-out for the school party, as he had no wish to incur further trouble by keeping them waiting.

"I say, Jen, what about Mr. Carter and Old Wilkie?" he asked anxiously. "They'll be hopping mad if we're away much longer."

"They'll have to hop, then: this is more important."

"M'yes, but all the same . . ." Darbishire shook his head doubtfully; then he went on: "I tell you what: *you*

79

look out for the thief, and *I'll* look out for Old Wilkie. After all, there'll be a frantic hoo-hah if we make them miss the bus."

The crowd by the gate was growing thicker every moment, as more and more people were streaming away from their seats. Mr. Findlater felt uneasy. How on earth could the boys hope to single out the man they wanted from a crowd like this?

"Give me the word at once, if you spot him," he encouraged them.

"Yes, sir; rather, sir."

It was a few moments later that Darbishire caught sight of Mr. Wilkins by the side of the scoring box. He was fidgeting with impatience, and it was clear from the expression on his face that he had already waited far longer than he thought necessary.

Darbishire was relieved to see him. Here was their chance to explain matters before the master's demeanour grew any worse!

"There he is!" he cried. "Waiting over there by himself."

"Where?" demanded Jennings and Mr. Findlater together.

Darbishire waved a hand in the direction of the scoring box. "Can't you see him? He's pacing up and down looking at his watch. We'd better go and tell him at once, before . . ."

"I see him! All right: leave this to me!"

There was a sudden movement at his side as R. J. Findlater, *Sussex* and *England*, streaked off on the trail of the quarry.

"Well, *I* can't see him," said Jennings. "The only character on the skyline over by the score box is Old Wilkie."

"Yes, of course! That's who I meant!"

"What!" Jennings gaped in astonishment. "You great, crumbling, addle-pated clodpoll, Darbishire—Old Wilkie isn't the thief!"

"I never said he was," Darbishire defended himself.

80

"*You're* supposed to be looking for the thief. I said *I'd* look out for Mr. Wilkins."

"Yes, but Mr. Findlater's never seen either of them: and now you've sent him belting off after Old Wilkie, by mistake. Honestly, Darbi, you must be as thick-skulled as a crash-helmet."

Darbishire's hand flew to his mouth in horror, as he realised what he had done.

"Oh, fish-hooks! I never thought of that. What a frantic bish! What had we better do, then?"

"We'd better go and jolly well rescue him before he gets clapped behind prison bars or something. Come on, Darbi; get moving. This is no time to hang about admiring the scenery."

The expedition for the liberation of Mr. Wilkins set off for the scoring box at a lively gallop, but the density of the crowd soon slowed their pace to an agitated crawl. They had not gone many yards when Jennings suddenly stopped and gripped his friend by the arm.

"Look, Darbi—just in front of us! It's the man who signed your book."

"Petrified paintpots! So it is! And look at his pockets—they're bulging like blinko!"

There was no doubt about it: they had stumbled upon their quarry quite by chance.

But what should they do? . . . For now they had found the thief they had lost Mr. Findlater, who was pounding after Mr. Wilkins like a bull on the trail of an unwary hiker.

Jennings made a quick decision.

"I'll follow this chap, while you run after Mr. Findlater and bring him back on the right scent."

"Yes, but what if——"

"Oh, go *on*, Darbi; don't waste time nattering. We don't want to lose him!" Jennings gave his friend a push to help him on his way, and then disappeared into the crowd.

Darbishire hurried forward on his errand, but as he approached the scoring box he was brought to a standstill by a scene that made his blood run chill with embarrassment . . . For the county player was holding Mr. Wilkins' arm in a restraining grip, while the master was protesting in flabbergasted amazement.

"I—I—Corwumph! This is monstrous. You must be off your head," Mr. Wilkins expostulated. "I assure you I've never been inside your pavilion in my life—let alone stolen anyone's possessions."

"We'll see about that," Mr. Findlater answered grimly. "The fact remains that you've been identified by two boys as the man they saw acting in a suspicious manner in the players' changing-room, shortly before the theft of certain valuables was discovered."

"Which boys? . . . What boys? . . . Where are these—these delinquent juveniles who make these fantastic charges against me?" demanded Mr. Wilkins, seething with indignation.

Mr. Findlater glanced over his captive's shoulder and caught sign of a small figure in the middle distance, hopping from foot to foot in agitation and dismay.

"Here's one of them coming now," he said.

Mr. Wilkins spun round to face his accuser. His jaw dropped: his eyes bulged with bewilderment, and his cheeks turned a delicate shade of pillar-box red. One strangled word of recognition forced its way through his vocal chords.

"*Darbishire!*" he gasped.

CHAPTER 9

TOKEN OF THANKS

CHARLES EDWIN JEREMY DARBISHIRE was never at his best when face to face with a crisis. He stood first on one leg, then on the other, twisting his fingers with confusion, and pink to the ears with shamefaced mortification.

"I'm terribly sorry, sir—I made a bish! I mean . . . I didn't mean . . . or rather . . ." The lame excuses faltered to a stop. How on earth could he explain?

By this time Mr. Findlater had realised that all was not well. Some hitch, it appeared, had occurred in the programme as advertised. He released his grip on Mr. Wilkins and asked: "Do you mean to say this isn't the right man?"

"Yes—I mean no, of course he isn't. That's Mr. Wilkins, one of our masters."

"You told me he was the thief!"

"What . . . what? . . . I—I—*Corwumph*!" fumed the indignant captive.

Darbishire avoided Mr. Wilkins' smouldering eye and mumbled: "Yes, I know, but I sort of got them mixed up, by mistake, if you see what I mean."

"Mistake?" echoed the cricketer in surprise. "Surely you know the difference between one of your masters and a—a bogus autograph forger!"

"Well, yes, of course I do, really."

"So I should hope," snorted Mr. Wilkins. "Considering the silly little boy has seen me every day for I don't know how long, it's about time he learnt to know me by sight!"

Slowly the explanation was pieced together, and Mr. Wilkins accepted the cricketer's apologies with as good a grace as he could muster. There remained, however, the problem of finding the real thief—a task which seemed almost impossible now that so much time had been wasted in trailing this unfortunate red herring.

"We'll never get him now. He'll have slipped out with the crowd and may be half a mile away," Mr. Findlater observed, while Darbishire kept his eyes on the ground and bit his lip in self-reproach. "Pity we missed him. He must have made a good haul, seeing he helped himself from the pockets of the whole team."

He turned to retrace his steps to the pavilion, and as he did so a youthful spectator disentangled himself from the throng milling round the gate, and came skipping towards them.

It was Jennings: and Darbishire's spirits sank still

further at the sight of his friend. For this could mean only that the shadower was returning to report his failure to keep the quarry under observation.

"What happened, Jen?" Darbishire asked, without enthusiasm.

"Well, I had a bit of bad luck, really," Jennings began. "I was following this chap when he looked round and saw me. He must have known I suspected him, because he dodged in and out of the crowd; and when he thought I wasn't looking he took cover in a little hut with lawn mowers and things inside."

"The groundsman's shed," confirmed Mr. Findlater. "If only you'd told me earlier, I could have nabbed him as he came out."

"I'm sorry, but I couldn't find you before, sir," Jennings apologised. "Actually, of course, the best thing would have been to have locked him in, but the last time I tried something like that it didn't work out very well."

"You mean to say you could have locked him in and you didn't do it!" Mr. Findlater chafed at the waste of such a golden opportunity.

"Well, no, I couldn't really, because there wasn't a key in the door. I was only thinking what I *could* have done if there *had* been."

"Never mind what you *could* have done. What *did* you do?" demanded Mr. Wilkins impatiently. "Just walked off and left the fellow to escape, I suppose?"

"Oh no, sir," Jennings replied. "I tried that dodge that General Merridew showed us the other week. There was a rolled-up cricket net leaning against the hut, so when the chap went in and shut the door I slipped the noose of the guy rope round the door handle, and tied it to a heavy roller that was standing just outside."

"You mean to say he's *still there*?" cried Mr. Findlater and Mr. Wilkins in unison.

"Oh, yes: that's what I came to tell you, sir. He can't get out till someone opens the door. Just like you and Mr. Carter, sir, when General Merridew took you prisoner in the library. Of course, I don't know if I did right, but . . ."

He broke off in mild surprise as he found that only Darbishire was left to listen to the story. The remaining two-thirds of his audience were pounding full-tilt towards the groundsman's hut.

Leading the field was R. J. Findlater, renowned for his speed between the wickets . . . Behind him galloped L. P. Wilkins, Esq., M.A. (Cantab.), less renowned as a sprinter, but grimly determined to reach the scene of operations before it was too late.

It took Mr. Carter some while to round up the missing members of the Linbury party. But at last they were all ready and set off for the bus stop in an excited, chattering crocodile.

Thus it was that they missed seeing the arrival of the police car which swung in through the gates of the county ground shortly after their departure. When the car left a few minutes later, the small thin man was sandwiched in the back seat between two policemen: the pockets of his shabby serge suit were bulging no longer.

The arrest was not spectacular. It was described by the ace crime reporter of the *Dunhambury Weekly Echo* in the words, "Later a man was detained."

All the way back to school, the Linbury boys could talk of nothing but the sensational climax of their holiday. The day's play had been well worth watching for its own sake; and with the addition of a hue and cry to enliven the proceedings, no one could complain that county cricket was a dull game to watch.

Only Darbishire remained quiet and thoughtful amongst the chattering crowd; and as the boys alighted near the school gates, Jennings sought the reason for his friend's silence.

"What are you looking so ossified about?" he inquired with kindly concern.

"My autograph book," replied Darbishire sadly. "It's
85

a mouldy chizz! All that hoo-hah and rushing about, and even *now* I haven't got R. J. Findlater's autograph!"

Darbishire need not have worried.

A week later the headmaster sent for both the boys to report to his study at the end of afternoon school.

The message was delivered by Binns and Blotwell, whom Mr. Pemberton-Oakes had intercepted while they were trotting off to the boot-lockers on a secret mission connected with the *Early Bedders' Guided Missiles Club*.

Upon his instructions, they altered course, and took a south-easterly bearing which led them to Classroom 3 where Jennings and Darbishire were putting away their books.

Blotwell switched on his imaginary transmitter and spoke in crisp, technical phrases.

"Hullo, Control! . . . Hullo Control! Space-Pilot Blotwell calling Jennings and Darbishire. Are you receiving me? . . . Are you receiving me? . . . Over!"

"What's up, Blotchy?" asked Jennings in non-technical language.

"Stand by for top-priority secret instructions from G.H.Q. Message begins: Archbeako orders Jennings and Darbishire to break off other engagements at once—*repeat* —at once—and report to base for top-level briefing. Zero hour sixteen-fifteen, British Standard Time . . . Over."

"Message received and understood," Jennings confirmed. "All the same, I wish I knew what he wanted us for. We haven't done anything wrong lately—well, *hardly* anything."

There was no cause for anxiety. Mr. Pemberton-Oakes was in the most kindly of moods when the boys reported to him in his study.

"I have received a letter from Mr. Findlater, the *England* cricketer, in connection with the—ah—unfortunate occurrence at the county ground last week," he told them.

Jennings and Darbishire opened their eyes wide in puzzled wonder. This was the last thing they had expected to hear.

"He says that it was mainly due to you two boys that the players did not have to go home with empty pockets; and as a token of thanks he would like you to accept the bat with which he scored his century that afternoon."

From behind his desk the headmaster produced a cricket bat and pointed to the long list of signatures inscribed on the blade. "It appears that the other players

have expressed a wish to be included in Mr. Findlater's—ah—generous gift, for you will notice that the bat bears the autographs of all the members of both teams."

Then the boys' eyes grew round as saucepan lids, and they flipped their fingers in delight.

"Ooh, sir . . . Thank you, sir . . . Thank you very much indeed, sir . . . !"

They hurried from the room, Jennings clutching the

precious bat, and Darbishire prancing alongside making imaginary late cuts and leg-glances at the empty air.

"I vote it belongs to both of us, in equal shares," Jennings suggested, when they had retired to a safe distance from the headmaster's study.

"Yes, of course; but what happens if we both want to use it at the same time?" Darbishire queried.

They gave some thought to the matter. Then Jennings said: "Well, how would it be if we said the bat was mostly mine, and the famous signatures were all yours. After all, I don't collect autographs, and the bat wouldn't be much use to you, really, because everyone knows you play cricket like a left-handed lobster, anyway."

Darbishire ignored the insult and agreed readily. The autographs of twenty-two first-class players was a prize worth having.

"That's fixed then," said Jennings. "Let's go and try it out on the cricket field and see how it goes."

There had been some rain that morning, and though a watery sun was now doing its best to dispel the scudding clouds, the grass was still wet underfoot when the boys arrived on the field. Here, they found Mr. Wilkins supervising an informal cricket practice, to occupy the half-hour before tea.

Atkinson, Bromwich and Martin-Jones were tossing a cricket ball to one another, but they abandoned their game and came hurrying across at Jennings' invitation to hear the good news and to inspect the precious bat at close quarters.

"Wow! Isn't it super!" crowed Atkinson.

"Yes: and it's the very same identical one that Findlater scored his hundred with that afternoon," Jennings announced proudly.

"And what's more, it's got twenty-two first-class autographs of famous sporting characters," Darbishire pointed out. "I reckon they look a jolly sight better on the actual bat than they would on the pink pages of my album."

For some moments a buzz of admiration arose

from the little group. Then Martin-Jones said: "Go into the net, Jen, and I'll give you a bowl to try it out."

"Righto. I'll pretend I'm opening the innings for England with my famous bat, eh?"

In point of fact the bat was two sizes too large for Jennings to use in comfort, but the glory of ownership more than made up for that. He patted the crease carefully, as Martin-Jones picked up the damp, slippery ball and commenced his run up to the wicket.

It was a good length ball, and the batsman stepped forward and smote it over the bowler's head with all his strength.

"Wacko! Super beefy swipe, Jen," approved Bromwich.

Then the trouble started . . .

As they stood following the flight of the ball, a sudden agonised cry rang out, and Darbishire came charging into the net, his eyes flashing danger signals and his cheeks quivering with woe.

"Hey! . . . Hi! . . . Whoa! . . . Stop, Jennings! Don't use it again whatever you do!"

They stared at him in surprise.

"Why not?" queried the batsman.

"Look what you've done to my autographs!"

Jennings glanced down at the bat. A round, red stain was clearly visible where the wet ball had made contact with the blade. Darbishire pointed to it in alarm.

"You mustn't use it for hitting with," he protested in horrified tones. "Every time you zonk a ball with it, you'll make dirty marks all over my nice clean autographs."

"I can't help that; it's just your bad luck," Jennings answered with a shrug. "Anyway, it won't be so bad when the ball's dry."

"Yes, it will. You'll wear them away, and then I shan't have any left. It isn't fair, hitting hard balls with famous autographs—or even soft ones, either."

It was not often that they saw Darbishire so moved to indignation, but now he bridled in defence of his rights like a mother hen protecting her brood.

"Oh, don't be so fussy," Jennings exclaimed impatiently. "What's the good of a bat if you can't use the thing? I've got a right to do what I like with my share of it. Besides, the signatures will probably wash off when we oil it, anyway."

"We aren't *going* to oil it," Darbishire maintained stubbornly.

"It won't be much good as a bat if we *don't*."

"It won't be much good as an autograph album if we *do*. Those sort of bats aren't meant to be used, I'd have you know."

"Of course they are," said Jennings. "You don't think Mr. Findlater's given it to us just so we can sit and stare at it during the long summer evenings, do you? Anyway, it's half mine and I'm jolly well going to use it."

"Well, the other half's mine, and I say you jolly well can't."

They had reached deadlock. They glared angrily at each other, all joy in their gift forgotten in this unhappy wrangle. Neither would yield an inch, and for some moments it seemed that their long-lasting friendship would founder on this rock of discord.

Oddly enough, it was Mr. Wilkins who saved the situation. He arrived at the cricket net to find Jennings and Darbishire red in the face with anger, and engaged in a bitter struggle. Jennings was holding the bat by the handle, while his adversary was doing all in his power to wrench it from his grasp.

"Now then, now then, you two! What's going on here?" the master demanded.

They told him.

"H'm," mused Mr. Wilkins . . . And for the second time within a fortnight his kind heart suggested a solution, at some cost to himself.

"What you really need is another bat to play with, so you can keep this one for exhibition purposes," he said.

"Yes, sir," said Jennings. "Of course, I *did* have another one, sir, only you confiscated it because—er—well, you know, sir."

Mr. Wilkins nodded. The episode of the chalky black-board duster still rankled in his mind. He had fully determined to retain the offending bat until the end of term. However . . .

"All right, then, Jennings. I'll give you your old one back," he said gruffly. "But if there's any more trouble about oiling it in the corridor, or bombarding people with chalky dusters, I'll—I'll—well, there had better not *be* any trouble."

"Yes, sir . . . No, sir . . . Thank you very much, sir," beamed Jennings.

The two boys turned to each other with sighs of joyful relief . . . Thanks to Mr. Wilkins' generous offer they could afford to be friends again.

CHAPTER 10

JENNINGS JUMPS TO CONCLUSIONS

THE CONFISCATED bat was returned the following morning; and much to Darbishire's relief Jennings agreed not to use Mr. Findlater's generous gift, except on rare and special occasions. Instead, the presentation bat with its priceless autographs was given a place of honour in the library. It stood on the bookcase next to the beady-eyed woodpecker in the glass case, and was greatly admired by the whole school.

The days sped by. Half-term week-end approached . . . and was gone almost before they had realised it: and with its passing, Mr. Carter's forecast about the waning interest in space-travel proved to be correct. True, there was still a certain amount of inter-planetary flight. From time to time an occasional rocket could be heard taking-off or landing on Jupiter or Venus, and odd bouts of space warfare were liable to break out while the junior forms were washing for lunch. But, by and large, the craze had passed its heyday, and the boys sought other pastimes to occupy their leisure moments.

Much of their free time was spent playing cricket. But by now swimming was on the daily programme as well, and this gave rise to exploits which were quite as fantastic as the out-moded games of space travel.

One did not need to be a strong swimmer to take part in daring adventures in or under the water. Neither Binns nor Blotwell could swim a stroke, but in spite of this handicap they formed a society known as the *Shallow-Enders' Frogmen's Union*—a band of lusty splashers who spent their pocket money on under-water goggles and rubber swimming-flippers.

Blotwell organised a team of human torpedoes to attack the ankles of more experienced swimmers who strayed into the shallow end of the swimming bath. Binns invented a method of breathing under water: with one end of a length of rubber tubing in his mouth, and the other end held above the surface with a stick, he would crawl across the bottom of the bath at a depth of two feet, and emerge choking, gasping and purple in the face. The breathing apparatus was finally confiscated by Mr. Carter as being a menace to all concerned.

The school's indoor swimming bath had been in use since the last week of May, but it was not until half-term had passed that the boys started practising in earnest for the inter-house swimming relay which always took place in the middle of July.

Jennings was a good swimmer, and he had been chosen to captain the *Drake* House junior team in its contest with the opposing house of *Raleigh*. Already in his mind he had picked the members of his team—Bromwich for the first lap, then Martin-Jones, then Pettigrew—a day boy from Form 3—and finally himself to provide the finishing spurt. He would like to have included Darbishire, but his friend's prowess in the water was a little uncertain.

At the beginning of the term, Darbishire had been nothing more than a land-lubberly splasher who bobbed up and down in the shallow end with the non-swimmers.

Lately, however, he seemed to have made remarkable progress. His name now appeared on the list of qualified swimmers, and, what is more, he had invented an entirely novel method of propelling himself through the water.

"Watch me, everybody," he announced, as he stood chest-deep in water in the swimming bath one Tuesday afternoon. "I will now demonstrate my famous new air-screw, paddle-steamer stroke."

"Go on, then, Darbi," encouraged Atkinson from the side of the bath. "We'll pull you out if you go under."

"Of course I shan't go under," retorted Darbishire. "This is an entirely new sort of contra-rotating butterfly stroke, with jet-propelled ankle movements. The important thing about it is that it leaves your hands free for—well, for scratching your head, or waving to spectators. Just you watch!"

He drew in a deep gulp of air and disappeared beneath the water. A moment later, a disturbance like a small-scale depth-charge showed that the demonstration was taking place. Every now and then a hand, a foot, or an elbow would break the surface as the swimmer trundled his way across the bath, like some clumsy sea-serpent performing a nightmare water-ballet.

"He's going jolly well, isn't he!" Atkinson remarked to Jennings, who had just climbed out of the water. "He zooms along just like a frogman."

"He's a bit small for a frogman: more like a tadpole-man, I'd say," Jennings replied. He cupped his hands to form a megaphone and shouted: "What about a spot of life-saving, Darbi? If I jump in, will you rescue me?"

For a moment the swimmer looked uncertain. Then he called back: "Righto, Jen; not too deep, though. Jump in near the three-foot-six mark and I'll tow you across."

Jennings went in with a splash that sent the water billowing over the coconut matting which covered the gangway. "Come and save me, then. I'll pretend I can't swim ... Help! Help!"

The rescuer flailed his way towards him. "Come a bit nearer, Jen; I can't reach you properly," he panted.

"What do you mean—'come nearer.'? I might be unconscious for all you know."

"Well, if you *were*, you wouldn't be shouting 'Help! Help!' at the top of your voice!"

Jennings found that he was well within his depth, so he put his feet on the bottom and registered a complaint.

"Look here, Darbi, if I've got to spend half an hour arguing about whether I'm unconscious or not, I'll be dead from frost-bite before you rescue me from drowning."

"All right, I've got you now," gasped the lifesaver, grabbing at Jennings' ears like a drowning man clutching at a straw. "Just keep calm and don't panic. Leave everything to me!"

"Who's panicking? I like the cheek of that!" protested the voluntary victim. "I can swim a jolly sight better than you, I'd have you know, and what's more . . . *Ach! Gll! Pff!*"

He broke off as his head was accidentally pushed beneath the surface by his well-meaning rescuer.

"Sorry, Jen," Darbishire apologised as his patient rose for air. "It's my famous patent paddle-steamer stroke. It's a jolly good one, of course, but it rather chucks the water about."

"You clumsy bazooka! You made me stub my toe on the bottom just then, and it's jolly painful," Jennings complained. "I thought you were supposed to be saving me, not drowning me."

"Yes, I know. That's what I *am* doing."

"Well, get on with it, while I'm still conscious, then. I shall be growing barnacles if I stay here much longer."

Jennings turned over on his back and Darbishire grasped him beneath the armpits and towed him slowly to the side.

The rescue was acclaimed with loud cheers by Atkinson and Martin-Jones, as they helped the life-saver to clamber back on to dry land.

"Jolly good, Darbi. A supersonic rescue, if ever I saw one," exclaimed Martin-Jones.

"Oh, it was nothing really," Darbishire replied modestly. "You wait till you see the new trudgeon stroke I'm inventing. It's specially designed to help channel swimmers in rough seas, and, what's more, it carries my personal guarantee."

Atkinson turned to Jennings who was sitting on the side of the bath nursing his injured toe. "How are you feeling after the famous rescue, Jen?"

"Oh, don't bother about my feelings—I'm only the chap who was drowning!" the victim complained.

Just then, Mr. Carter blew the whistle and the swimmers came scrambling out of the bath and dripped their way into the changing cubicles which lined the wall on one side.

A few moments later the touselled head of the *Drake* House junior swimming captain appeared round the door of Darbishire's cubicle.

"I say, Darbi, I've been thinking," Jennings began. "Your swimming's been coming on like a house on fire lately, and I've a jolly good mind to put you down as first-length reserve for the relay."

Darbishire paused in the act of slipping his shirt over his still damp shoulders. "Who, me? . . . Oh no, really, Jen. I'm not nearly good enough."

"Your life-saving's a menace to shipping, I admit, but that gyroscopic paddle-steamer stroke, or whatever you call it, would be just the job to get us a lead on the first lap. Of course, you won't be needed unless Bromwich catches lumbago, or something, but it's as well to have a reserve, just in case."

A look of alarm passed over Darbishire's features as he picked up his spectacles from the floor and cleaned them on his swimming trunks.

"You—er—you don't think Bromo *is* sickening for anything, do you?" he asked in a strained, unnatural voice.

"Oh, gosh, no!"

"Thank goodness for that!"

"Bromo will be all right, don't you worry. I just thought

I'd tell you because—well, because it's a jolly lobsterous honour to be picked as a reserve, isn't it?"

Jennings returned to his own cubicle, limping a little, for his stubbed toe was still painful. While he was dressing he decided to go and see Matron and ask her for a piece of sticking-plaster with which to protect the slight injury from further damage. That, at any rate, would be his excuse; though the truth was that he always enjoyed a chat with Matron whenever he could think of some excuse for paying her a visit.

He was not the only boy who made a practice of dropping in to her sitting-room at odd moments. Most of the boarders—and the staff too—found Matron a sympathetic person who would always do her best to help them with their daily problems. And even as Jennings was mounting the stairs to her room, she was busy coping with her latest problem—a little matter brought to her attention by Mr. Wilkins.

"I wonder if you'd help me, Matron," Mr. Wilkins had said when he had arrived at her sitting-room a few minutes earlier. "An old friend of mine is getting married on Saturday week, and the headmaster's given me leave to go up to London the day before, and stay for the wedding."

Mr. Wilkins' problem concerned the suit which he was hoping to wear for the ceremony. As soon as he had received the invitation, he had journeyed to Brighton and ordered a new suit to be made to measure. The tailor had assured him that the work would be put in hand without delay, and that the suit would be despatched as soon as it was ready. All the same, he could not promise that it would arrive earlier than the midday post on the Friday of Mr. Wilkins' departure.

"It's an awful nuisance. It should come in time, but it may not," he explained. "I was hoping to go up to town first thing on the Friday morning. It seems a pity to hang around waiting for the postman. You see, I've got to be back here in time for school on the following Monday morning."

"That's all right, Mr. Wilkins," Matron replied. "Let me know where you're staying on the Friday night, and if the parcel doesn't come before you go, I'll forward it on to you."

"Thank you, Matron; that's very good of you."

It was then that a knock sounded on the door, and Jennings limped painfully into the room.

"Oh, please, Matron, I've stubbed my toe and I'm in ghastly agony—honestly, Matron," he announced in tragic tones.

Matron was sorry to hear it. "Come in and sit down, Jennings. I'm busy at the moment." She turned again to Mr. Wilkins and said: "Let me make sure I've got this right. You'll definitely be leaving here on Friday week—is that so?"

"That's right, Matron," he replied jovially, searching in his pocket for a scrap of paper on which to write the address of his hotel. "First train after breakfast, and by jove! I shan't be sorry to go. Somebody else can cope with Form 3, and I hope they enjoy it!"

"Oh, don't say that," she replied with a smile. "I expect Form 3 will be sorry to lose you. Don't you agree, Jennings?"

But Jennings could only gape in astonishment at what he had just heard.

So Mr. Wilkins was leaving! After all these years at Linbury he had decided to make a change. It was incredible! . . . Unbelievable! And yet it must be true, for had not the master just confirmed the tidings with his own lips?

What a good thing it was, Jennings thought, that he had been on hand to hear of the forthcoming departure . . . For this was important news that must be acted upon without delay!

It was well known at Linbury Court that whenever there was a red herring to be trailed, or a wrong conclusion to be drawn, Jennings was the right person for the job.

Here was a case in point. If only he had taken the

trouble to inquire, Matron could have told him that Mr. Wilkins would be returning in time for school on the Monday following his departure.

But Jennings did not inquire. Instead, heedless of his injured toe, he rushed off post-haste to the Common Room to broadcast the news of the master's resignation.

"I say, have you chaps heard? Super priority hush-hush, stop-press, news-bulletin!" he announced to the crowd as he hurtled through the door with the force of a rugger forward breaking loose from the scrum. "You'll never guess what it is!"

The Common Room was crowded with boys waiting for the tea bell. They looked at Jennings with scant interest.

"I bet it's something feeble—like kippers for tea," said Temple scathingly.

"No, it isn't, it's—well—I'll tell you. *Mr. Wilkins is leaving!*"

There followed a few seconds of stupefied silence while the unexpected tidings sank in. Then there arose a babble of disbelief.

"Old Wilkie leaving! Don't be so stark raving cuckoo, Jennings . . . You're pulling our legs!"

"Don't you believe him," Venables warned the crowd. "According to Jennings there's always some sort of supersonic hoo-hah brewing up, and it never comes to anything."

"Well, this time it's true," Jennings maintained. "If you don't believe me, you can jolly well ask Matron. I heard him tell her which train he was going on, and what's more, she's got his address so she can send his things on to him."

They believed him then: first, because his tone was so earnest, and secondly because startling rumour is always more exciting than sober truth. Besides, if Matron knew all about it, it *must* be true.

At first the news was received with unrestrained joy.

"Hooray! . . . Wacko! . . . Yippee! . . ." Sounds of rejoicing could be heard all over the room.

"No more maths tests on Fridays," cried Atkinson,

cavorting round the Common Room table in an improvised war dance.

"I'm jolly glad he's going. I never did like Old Wilkie much," Venables asserted. "Always getting in a bate and blowing up like a hydrogen bomb about nothing at all."

"Hear, hear," added Temple. "Let's hope we get someone decent for a change, when he's gone."

By bed time their mood had changed. Mr. Wilkins had his faults—that was agreed. But who could tell whether the new master who would come to take his place might not be even more difficult to get on with! It was foolish to prattle about the end of maths tests on Fridays. Why, for all they knew, this new man might keep their noses glued to their maths books morning, noon and night.

"I'm jolly sorry he's leaving," Martin-Jones remarked as he undressed in Dormitory 6 that evening. "You've got to admit he's pretty decent, except when he's in bate."

"I'm sorry, too," said Venables. "I always liked him, really."

"You said this afternoon you were glad," Darbishire reminded him.

"Ah, yes; but that was before I remembered that the new character might be a jolly sight worse."

It was then that Jennings had a bright idea.

"I reckon we ought to buy Old Wilkie a little present, just to show him how sorry we are that he's going," he suggested.

The bright idea was taken up with enthusiasm.

"I'll subscribe sixpence," Venables offered.

"I've got an unused stamp you can have," volunteered Atkinson.

"If my postal order comes this week, I'll fork out ninepence," said Bromwich generously.

Within a few minutes it had become obvious that the *Mr.-Wilkins'-Farewell-Gift-Fund* would have to be organised on a proper footing. So a committee was appointed to collect the contributions and decide upon a suitable present.

"I vote for Jennings as Chairman, because it was his

idea, and Darbishire as Hon. Sec. and Treasurer, because he's got a decent money-box," Temple proposed. "Hands up all characters who agree."

A dozen hands shot into the air.

"Hey, you can't vote for yourself, Jennings—that's not fair," Atkinson objected.

"Why not? I think I'd make a rather decent Chairman," Jennings argued. "Anyway, no one's voted against us, so that means Darbi and I are carried anonymously—er—umanimously—well, anyway, we've won twelve-nil, so that settles it."

Bristling with eagerness, the Chairman turned to the Hon. Sec. and said: "We'll get everything organised first thing to-morrow. Send out notices signed by the Chairman, Secretary and Treasurer, to say there'll be a committee meeting after breakfast to decide how best to make chaps fork out contributions."

"Send out notices?" echoed the Secretary. "Who shall I send them to? Dash it all, Jen, there's only you and me on the committee and we know about it already!"

The Chairman was not going to allow his methods to be questioned by junior members of his staff.

"Listen, Darbi," he said in tones of patient rebuke, "I've just been voted Chairman of this outfit after a keenly fought contest, and I'm going to do the job properly. Make out three notices signed by both of us. Then give one to me and keep the other two yourself."

"Why two?"

"You're Secretary *and* Treasurer, aren't you? Very well, then: one for each department."

"Just as you say, Mr. Chairman," replied the Hon. Sec. obediently.

Everyone in Dormitory 6 felt a little easier in their minds after that. A farewell gift would do much to make up for all the trouble they had caused Mr. Wilkins in the past: and while they undressed they debated how they could cheer up his last ten days at Linbury. Perhaps, if they were unusually kind and thoughtful, they could spread a little sunshine across the shadow of his departure.

Venables sat up in bed twirling his dressing-gown cord round like a propeller, and wishing he had worked harder in Mr. Wilkins' lessons.

"I bet he'll be sorry he left us when he gets to this new school he's going to," he observed. "I bet the chaps there won't be half so decent to him as we've been—or rather as we're *going* to be!"

"Hear, hear! But what I want to know is, how can we be *more* decent to him than we are already?" queried Atkinson.

"Oh, lots of ways," Jennings answered. "Open the door for him when he goes out of the room."

"I always do that, anyway."

"Well, open it wider, then . . . And laugh whenever he cracks a joke."

"I always do that, too."

"Well, laugh louder, then. I know Old Wilkie's jokes are a bit chronic, but the least we can do is to pretend they're funny. It won't cost you anything to laugh in a good cause, will it!"

Outside on the landing, the duty master's voice could be heard booming out a warning to a neighbouring dormitory about the importance of washing behind both ears.

"He's coming!" Jennings announced, picking his pyjama jacket from the floor with the toes of his left foot. "Don't forget—all be specially decent to him from now on."

When Mr. Wilkins reached Dormitory 6, he was somewhat surprised by the warmth of the reception that awaited him. Instead of the usual disorderly turmoil, he found that everyone—except Jennings—was already in bed, and favouring him with sad, sweet smiles that would have done credit to Little Lord Fauntleroy.

At once his suspicions were aroused. Such perfect behaviour could only mean that some mischief was afoot. He glanced round the room but could see nothing amiss, so he turned sharply on the one boy who was still out of bed.

"Quickly now, Jennings," he ordered. "I'm tired of

standing about in draughty dormitories waiting for you stragglers to get into bed."

Darbishire switched off his sweet smile, and replaced it with a look of tender sympathy.

"You're tired, sir? Would you like to sit down, sir? You can sit on my bed if you like, sir," he offered.

"No, sit on mine, sir," begged Temple. "My mattress isn't so lumpy as Darbishire's."

Mr. Wilkins was puzzled. This concern for his comfort was unusual to say the least! And his bewilderment increased when Jennings skipped across to the window and tugged on the cord that raised the sash.

"What on earth are you doing, boy?" the master demanded.

"Closing the window, sir. You said it was draughty in the dormitories, sir. You might catch a cold if you sat in a draught, sir."

"I—I—! Go back to bed at once, you silly little boy. Never mind about my catching cold: but if you aren't in bed in two seconds from now, Jennings, you'll catch it hot!"

It was not intended to be a humorous remark, but so great was their desire to please that the boys seized upon this so-called gem of wit and savoured it to the full.

"Oh, sir! . . . I say, you chaps, did you hear that?" exclaimed Jennings in delight. "Mr. Wilkins has made a joke! 'Don't catch cold, or you'll catch it hot' . . . Jolly witty answer, sir! I wish I could think of things like that!"

Waves of exaggerated laughter billowed round the room as the boys sat in bed rocking with counterfeited glee.

"Ha! ha! ha!" roared Bromwich, his eyes swimming with bogus tears of mirth. "Supersonic joke, sir. You ought to be on television, sir!"

"Yes, rather," agreed Temple, between gasp of hilarity. "I must remember to put that in my letter home next week. 'You can catch cold, but you can't catch hot.' Ha, ha, ha!"

"Silence!" thundered Mr. Wilkins: and immediately

"Go back to bed, Jennings," ordered Mr. Wilkins

the laughter stalled in mid-burst. "Stop that silly noise, all of you. It wasn't meant to be a joke, anyway."

"No, but it was jolly clever, all the same, sir," said Jennings with deep appreciation, as he climbed between the sheets.

Mr. Wilkins felt vaguely uneasy as he put out the dormitory light and went downstairs to the staff room. Here he found Mr. Carter, in whom he confided his worries.

"I say, Carter, Dormitory 6 have gone completely off their heads," he began. "They're so amazingly polite that I think there's some sort of jiggery-pokery going on."

Mr. Carter raised an interested eyebrow. "Surely you aren't *complaining* because they're well behaved, are you?" he asked.

"No, no, of course not. But I ask you, Carter, is it natural that a boy like Jennings should feel worried in case I was standing in a draught?"

Mr. Carter agreed that he hadn't heard of such a thing happening before.

"And another thing. I made a rather feeble joke, and they all roared their heads off as though it was the funniest thing they'd ever heard."

"Really! What did you say?"

Mr. Wilkins hesitated. He felt diffident about repeating his modest quip in cold blood.

"Oh, it was nothing, really. I just told Jennings that whether or not I caught cold, he would catch it hot if he didn't get a move on."

Mr. Carter waited, expecting more. "Well, go on. What was the joke?" he asked.

"That was it. That's what I said," Mr. Wilkins explained, with a self-conscious laugh.

For a moment his colleague looked blank. Then, in tones of mock admiration, he said: "Oh, I see. Yes, of course. Very witty of you, Wilkins. In fact, I wonder you don't . . ."

"All right, all *right*! I told you it wasn't all that funny," Mr. Wilkins protested. "But what beats me is why those silly little boys thought it *was*."

"If you ask me, I'd say they were having you on," Mr. Carter decided. "All this concern for your welfare sounds suspiciously like a leg-pull."

Mr. Wilkins bristled angrily. "That's just what I thought," he said. "And what's more, I'm not going to stand for it. If anyone else goes out of his way to be pleasant, there's going to be trouble."

"You can't discourage politeness and good manners," his colleague pointed out.

"Well, you know what I mean. I shall watch those boys pretty closely for the next few days," Mr. Wilkins retorted. "And if I find any more disgraceful exhibitions of —of extremely courteous conduct, I'll—I'll—well, they'd better look out!"

CHAPTER 11

DARBISHIRE'S SECRET

JENNINGS SPENT most of his free time during the next two days in collecting donations for Mr. Wilkins' Farewell Gift.

Most of the boys gave him threepence, because they were sorry that the master was leaving: a few subscribed sixpence because they were glad, and felt they were getting good value for their money.

On Thursday evening, when just a week remained before Mr. Wilkins' reported departure, the Chairman and Secretary of the Presentation Committee held a further meeting in Classroom 3, to discuss their future plans. First, they poured out on to a desk all the money they had collected: it amounted to eighteen shillings and ninepence, including postal orders and stamps.

"We haven't done too badly, have we, Darbi?" Jennings observed. "I'll give one and threepence out of my pocket money to make it up to a round pound."

"Jolly nimble," beamed the Hon. Sec. and Treasurer. "The next thing, now, is what we're going to buy him. I'd thought of something like an umbrella stand, only then we'd have to give him an umbrella to put in it, and Old Wilkie always wears a raincoat, anyway."

"It ought to be something that makes him think of us every time he looks at it," the Chairman observed, peering round the room in search of inspiration. "Something like—well, say, a rather decent wastepaper basket, or a manicure set."

"We ought to have it engraved, too—whatever we decide upon," said Darbishire. He took a sheet of writing paper from his desk and spent some minutes in composing a suitable inscription. When he had done so, he said with modest pride: "How about this, Jen! Listen—Presented to L. P. Wilkins, Esq., M.A., by the boys of Linbury Court School in memory of many years' faithful service, and hoping you will be able to pop over and see us again some time, if you aren't too busy!"

"Too long," was Jennings' verdict. "We'd never be able to scratch all that on a manicure set. Besides, I've just remembered he's got a pair of nail scissors already."

It was not easy to think of a suitable gift, and they spent the next half-hour making wildly unsuitable suggestions which ranged from a gross of pipe-cleaners to a chromium-plated nutmeg-grater.

Finally Jennings said: "Of course, if we can't think of anything else, we could always buy him his ticket to London; but that's not much of a present to remember us by, is it!"

Venables wandered into the classroom to see what progress the committee had made.

"If it was me who was leaving, I know what I'd like," he said, when he heard of their difficulties.

"What?" asked Jennings, with rising hope.

"Well, I'd like a signal-box for my model railway."

The Chairman thumped the desk with exasperation. "But Mr. Wilkins hasn't *got* a model railway, you bat-witted clodpoll!"

"I never said he had," Venables argued. "I said, if *I* was in *his* place, and it was *me* who was leaving . . ."

"Oh, go *away*, Venables," Jennings exclaimed impatiently. "You're not supposed to be butting in at all, really. This is a private selection committee meeting, I'd have you know."

"All right, all right, I'm going. But I bet you make a bish of the whole issue without me to advise you," Venables prophesied. "According to you, Jennings, nobody else knows . . ."

The Chairman threw a geography book at the interrupter and the meeting proceeded in peace.

But not for long . . . For a few moments later Mr. Wilkins' voice was heard just outside in the corridor, and in wild alarm Jennings and Darbishire began scooping up the coins from the desk and dropping them back into the money-box.

"Oh, fish-hooks! If he sees all this cash lying about he'll guess what's up," Jennings exclaimed. Hurriedly he replaced the last of the coins, and then glanced round the room for some place of concealment.

"Open the cupboard quick, Darbi," he ordered in a voiceless whisper. "I don't suppose Old Wilkie will ever think of poking his head in there."

"Jennings!"

The boy wheeled round at the sound of his name, to find Mr. Wilkins standing in the doorway glowering at him.

"What did I hear you saying then?" the master demanded.

"Nothing, sir—or rather . . ." Jennings shifted his feet uncomfortably. What on earth could he say? The news of the farewell gift must be kept a secret until the proper time arrived.

"Come along boy; no nonsense, now. What was that remark you were making about Old—er—about me, as I came in?"

"I was just saying that I didn't suppose you'd want to put your head in the cupboard, sir.

Mr. Wilkins' complexion turned three shades pinker. "Put my head in the cupboard!" he echoed.

"I think Jennings meant that it wouldn't be a very comfortable place to put it, sir," Darbishire added helpfully.

By this time Mr. Wilkins was convinced that the cupboard held the answer to whatever practical joke was being planned at his expense. Without a second glance at the tell-tale money-box on the desk, he strode across the room and flung the cupboard door wide open.

Orderly rows of text books met his gaze; and though he carried out a thorough search, he could find nothing to confirm the suspicions that had first been aroused in him in the dormitory two evenings before.

Mr. Wilkins was baffled. *Something* was in the wind! Some deep-laid jiggery-pokery was being planned at his expense. He was sure of that, for otherwise there was no explanation for the exaggerated politeness, the tender sympathy and the smiles of welcome that had greeted him all over the building during the last couple of days. What was it all leading up to? He didn't know, but he meant to find out . . . Oh, yes, *he'd* find out right enough, as sure as his name was L. P. Wilkins! For the moment, however, he would hold his peace and keep his eyes open for the key to the mystery.

Angry and bewildered, he slammed the cupboard door and strode from the room without another word.

"Phew! That was a near one," Jennings sighed in relief, as soon as the master was out of earshot. "It's jolly dangerous trying to be decent to Old Wilkie. He makes it just about as awkward as he can!"

"Yes, I know," Darbishire agreed. "And the more we try to cheer him up the worse bates he gets into. I offered him my last liquorice allsort this morning, and gave him a stately bow when I opened the door specially wide for him; and all he said was that he didn't want any more of my insolence, thanks very much."

"I dare say he's fed up because he's got to leave us tomorrow week," Jennings decided. "The only thing we can do is to turn the other cheek and go on being more decent to him than ever. Whatever happens, he mustn't guess that we know he's going, or that'll spoil the big surprise when we dish his present out to him."

The dormitory bell sounded then, so the committee was obliged to postpone its discussion, and it was not until break the next morning that a definite decision was reached about the farewell gift.

Then, Jennings rushed up to Darbishire as he was drinking his mid-morning milk, and slapped him on the back in triumph.

"Listen, Darbi, I've had a supersonic brainwave—it came to me suddenly during arithmetic," he announced. "How about a clock?"

"Golly, yes. Just the job," Darbishire agreed, his eyes lighting up behind his milk-splashed spectacles.

"I expect they've got some decent ones at that shop in the village," Jennings went on. "So if I get permission to go into Linbury and buy it next Wednesday, we could show it to all the chaps first, and then dole it out to Old Wilkie when he takes us for English on Thursday afternoon. It'll be his very last lesson with us before he leaves."

"Righto, then. And somebody ought to make a speech to go with it, if we're not going to have that inscription," Darbishire suggested. "You can't just bung it over and say—'Here you are.' "

"Bags you make the speech, then."

"Who, me? Oh, fish-hooks, I shouldn't know what to say," Darbishire demurred.

"That doesn't matter. No one will be listening, anyway. Just stand up and woffle like the old geezers who dole out the prizes on Speech Day."

Darbishire considered the matter, and finally decided that this important part of the ceremony could safely be entrusted to him. He had the best part of a week before him in which to think of a few well-chosen remarks, and he planned to use his spare time in preparing a speech worthy of the occasion.

Unfortunately, two things happened during the week-end which threw this plan into confusion, and filled his waking moments with alarm.

First, the swimming bath was placed out of bounds, in order that Robinson, the odd-job man, could re-paint the interior woodwork before the junior inter-house swimming relay was held the following Friday afternoon.

This would have had little bearing upon the events which followed, had not Bromwich retired to bed with a bad cold on Sunday, which gave rise to a rumour that he might not be well enough to swim for his House when the great day dawned. Under the circumstances, it seemed that Jennings had acted wisely in choosing a reserve to fill the vacant place.

There was no shortage of swimmers in *Drake* House, but in order to encourage the novices, the headmaster had made it a rule that the first lap in the junior relay should be undertaken by those who had learnt to swim during the current term; and apart from Bromwich, Darbishire was the only junior in his House to fulfil this condition.

By the following morning the rumour had grown into news. Jennings heard about it during break, but even so he was not unduly worried at the prospect of having to make a change in his team.

After all, Darbishire's recent improvement as a swimmer, his patent paddle-steamer stroke and his demonstrations of gyroscopic ankle-movements had been remarked upon throughout the school. Unaware of the shock that awaited him, the junior swimming captain trotted off to find his friend and congratulate him upon his good fortune.

He found Darbishire in the library, looking up Latin quotations to use in his forthcoming speech. He was wearing his spectacles high up on his forehead, a habit of his when deep in thought.

"I say, Darbi, what do you think?" Jennings began. "Matron's put Bromo off swimming because of his cold, and you'll probably have to take his place in the relay."

The effect upon Darbishire was remarkable. His mouth fell open and his eyebrows shot up, sending his spectacles

110

slithering down on to his nose where they perched crookedly like a percentage sign. He gulped and swallowed hard.

"Oh no, Jen, not me," he protested in dismay. "I'd much rather not—honestly."

"There's no one else. Anyway, you ought to be jolly pleased. It's your big chance to show everyone how well you can do your famous jet-propelled side-stroke. or whatever you call it. You were saying only the other day how fast you could go."

"Yes, I know, but . . ."

Darbishire broke off helplessly, and gazed into the middle distance with staring, troubled eyes. It seemed that something was on his mind which he would dearly like to confess, if only he could bring himself to do so.

Most of this escaped Jennings' notice, and he prattled on gaily, unaware of his friend's anxiety. "Yes, you'll only have Thompson swiming against you, so if you can give us a decent send-off in the first lap, we ought to pretty well walk away with the rest."

"Walk away!" Darbishire echoed gloomily. "We can't very well walk in the deep end, can we?"

Jennings looked at him sharply. Darbishire ought to be cavorting with joy at his good fortune, instead of moping and moaning in this miserable fashion. Whatever was the matter with the lad?

"For goodness' sake stop looking so fossilised, Darbi," he said sternly. "I'm offering you a place in the team and a chance to swim for your House. Don't you realise what that means?"

Darbishire nodded. "Yes, I know, Jen, but there's something I ought to tell you. There's just one ghastly snag about putting me in the swimming team. You see, I . . ."

His courage failed him and he stopped short.

"Well, go on," Jennings prompted.

The words came at last, slowly and with obvious effort. "Well, you see, it's like this, Jen, I . . . *I can't swim!*"

CHAPTER 12

TROUBLED WATERS

JENNINGS STARED at Darbishire in amazement.

"You can't swim?" he echoed, aghast.

"Well, I *can* swim—a little bit," Darbishire explained. "I'm all right in the shallow end, but I can't go out of my depth because I have to put one foot on the bottom every three strokes."

"But that's crazy!"

"No, it's not. It's a jolly good scheme if you don't want to go under."

"I mean I just can't believe it," said Jennings faintly. And indeed, there was every excuse for his stunned incredulity. Why, only two days before, Darbishire had been proudly demonstrating to the shallow-end frogmen his guaranteed technique for assisting channel-swimmers in rough seas: furthermore, he had offered to teach Binns and Blotwell how to master the crawl stroke in six easy lessons.

Now, however, he merely looked sheepish. when reminded of the enthusiasm with which his offer had been received.

"Oh, that! Well you see, I was only pretending," he mumbled.

"Pretending!" Jennings could hardly believe his ears.

"Well, it's jolly rotten if everyone else can swim and you can't. Makes you feel out of it," Darbishire defended himself. "Anyway, it wasn't my fault to start with."

According to Darbishire, Mr. Wilkins was the real cause of the trouble, for it was he who had accidentally added the boy's name to the list of swimmers when it should, by rights, have remained on the list of beginners.

Every week or so, the novices who were learning to swim were tested to see what progress they had made. As soon as they could swim the whole length of the bath with ease, their names were added to the list of capable swimmers who were allowed to use the deep end. New lists appeared at intervals, and it was due to some error in compiling the latest batch of names that Darbishire found himself favoured with an honour which he did not deserve. He had been so proud and delighted at this unexpected promotion, that he had not been able to bring himself to point out the mistake.

So far, the little deception had worked surprisingly well. By proceeding down the bath until he was chin-deep in water, he had been able to conceal the fact that his more brilliant strokes were made while he was still within his depth. It was a help, he admitted, that the water was usually somewhat cloudy.

Jennings listened to the confession with shocked indignation.

"Gosh. what a frantic fraud you are, Darbi," he said when the tale was told. "And you even had the cheek to life-save *me*. Why, I might have been drowned!"

Darbishire hastened to reassure him. "Oh no, Jen. You were in your depth, don't forget: and besides, *you* can swim anyway."

"Well, in that case I didn't need rescuing," Jennings replied with youthful logic. "And all that woffle about keeping calm and not panicking and leaving everything to you! You might as well own up, Darbi; you're a bogus, gruesome swizzler, and you haven't a leg to stand on."

"Not *now*, perhaps," Darbishire admitted, "but I had a leg to stand on when I was doing my famous strokes. That's what made them look so nimble."

Jennings clicked his teeth in exasperation. "But what are we going to do about the relay? You can't take part in a swimming race hopping along with one foot on the bottom—not in the deep end, anyway."

"Well, I might be able to manage it if I had some more practice," Darbishire said hopefully. "I can go quite decently in the shallow end. It's just that when I go deeper, the bottom seems such a long way down if you've never swum over it before."

113

So there and then they decided that Jennings should give Darbishire some intensive coaching, to enable him to swim the full length of the bath.

Clearly, there was no time to be lost! They must devote the whole of the following day's swimming period to this urgent task . . . And then they remembered that the bath had been placed out of bounds, and that there would be no more swimming until the decorations had been completed.

"That puts the tin lid on it, then," Darbishire lamented.

But Jennings was not to be defeated so easily. "Don't be such a feeble specimen," he argued. "What's to stop us popping in there after prep. this evening?"

"Someone might see us pop," Darbishire pointed out.

"Not if we're careful. I'll get Atkinson to come along and keep watch. There'll just be time for a lesson before the dorm. bell goes."

Darbishire was still uneasy. "I don't think it's safe. I don't like the idea of going out of my depth without Mr. Carter, or someone, being there," he confessed.

"Don't worry; I'll look after you," Jennings replied, with all the confidence of a capable life-saver. "*Some* people, Darbi—and when I say *some* people I mean me, myself, personally—*some* people know how to life-save other people without keeping one foot on the bottom all the time."

The rebuke was well deserved. "Sorry, Jen," Darbishire muttered humbly.

Directly after evening preparation the two boys crept furtively into the swimming bath, while Atkinson kept watch outside the door.

The building reeked of wet paint, for Robinson had applied the first coat that afternoon. and had left the door and windows open in order that it should dry more quickly.

Darbishire had some difficulty in changing into his swimming trunks without touching the freshly painted white walls and green woodwork; but at last he was ready, and emerged from his cubicle wearing a pair of green rubber frogs'-feet attached to his ankles.

He had borrowed these swimming flippers from Temple,

as he thought that they would give him more confidence to face the dangers of the deep end. Unfortunately, in his nervous haste, he had fastened them on the wrong feet, and this rather impeded his progress as he flipped and flapped his way along the coconut matting to the shallow end of the bath.

"Brr! It looks jolly cold," he complained, dipping his flipper into the water in an effort to gauge the temperature.

"Oh, go on in, if you're going," said Jennings impatiently. "We haven't got time to hang about while you stand there shivering your timbers and square-dancing in your frogs'-feet . . . And take your glasses off—they won't be a bit of good without windscreen wipers."

"I was going to pretend they were frogmen's goggles," Darbishire explained.

He removed his glasses, placed them on the floor at the end of the bath, and lowered himself gingerly into the water.

"Wow! Brr! It's freezing! This isn't going to do my chilblain any good, I'd have you know."

"Start swimming towards the deep end," Jennings ordered. "No, no, no—not like that. Take your foot off the bottom!"

"I haven't g-got going yet," Darbishire mumbled through chattering teeth. "I think it's the smell of that w-wet p-paint. It's p-putting me off my s-stroke."

"You haven't *done* a stroke for it to put you off yet, so don't make feeble excuses," said the instructor acidly. "Pretend you're a channel swimmer—they don't give up just because of the smell of wet paint."

"There isn't any w-wet p-paint in the Channel. Why, for all you know . . ."

"Oh, for goodness' sake get on with it! Shoot your arms forward and kick your legs properly."

The lesson proceeded by fits and starts, and soon the swimmer gained confidence and swam a full eight strokes across the width of the shallow end without once running aground.

"Jolly nimble," Jennings encouraged him. "Do that once more, and you'll be ready to try a bit deeper."

But Darbishire had thought of a new excuse to delay the fateful moment.

"Yes, but look here," he protested. "If I get stuck in the deep end, you'll have to jump in and rescue me, and you haven't got your swimming things on."

"Wow! I'd forgotten about that! You'd better wait while I go and get them."

"But I can't wait to be saved if I'm out of my depth!"

"No, you clodpoll! I mean, stay where you are now, in the shallow end, while I nip into the cloakroom and fetch my trunks."

An icy chill spread through Darbishire's damp limbs, and he shivered like a blancmange on a fast-moving dinner-trolley.

"Oh fish-hooks! I shall freeze. I shall need thawing out with a blow-lamp if I've got to hang about here all that time."

He was saved from this frosty fate by a sudden turn of events which threatened to prove even more alarming. For no sooner had he finished speaking, than Atkinson came hurrying in through the door waving his arms in frantic gestures of warning.

"Look out! . . . Look out! Out of the bath quick, Darbishire! . . . Mr. Carter and Old Wilkie are heading this way across the quad."

The swimming lesson broke up in turmoil and confusion, as Darbishire floundered clumsily back to the side, urged on by Atkinson's panic-stricken signals of haste. Then he and Jennings helped to pull the swimmer out of the water, where he stood dripping and shivering in an agony of guilty dismay.

"Quick, quick! They'll be here in a minute," gasped Atkinson. "We'll have to hide in here, somewhere. They'll see us if we try to go out through the door."

"Oh, goodness, this is frantic! There'll be the most supersonic hoo-hah if we're copped out of bounds," Darbishire wailed.

Jennings took command. Seizing the reluctant swimmer by the wrist, he led the way to the nearest changing cubicle.

"All get in here and crouch down. They won't spot us if we shut the door," he whispered.

"But it's all sticky wet paint in there," moaned Darbishire. "I had a gruesome job not to touch it while I . . ."

Jennings propelled him inside with a slight push. Atkinson followed, and the three boys crouched down behind the door in a damp and uncomfortable huddle.

"Stop shivering, Darbi," Jennings whispered. "They'll hear your teeth chattering at the other end of the bath . . . And budge up a bit—you're shoving me against the wall."

"I haven't got r-room to b-budge up!" Darbishire protested. "I've hardly got room to sh-hiver pr-properly. And what's more, I—I—I . . ."

His chattering teeth clattered to a halt as the sound of footsteps was heard approaching from the far end of the building.

It was Mr. Carter who had suggested strolling over to the swimming bath, to see what progress Robinson had made with his work of decoration. Mr. Wilkins had agreed readily. Normally, the two masters shared the work of supervising swimming for the school, though they had arranged that Mr. Carter should organise the junior relay as Mr. Wilkins would be away on his week-end leave when the event took place. The senior event, which had resulted in a win for *Drake,* had been decided the previous week, and the masters were discussing the forthcoming junior race as they crossed the quad and entered the supposedly empty building.

For several minutes they sauntered to and fro, admiring the green and white paint-work, and quite unaware of the havoc that their presence was causing inside the furthermost cubicle.

Presently, Mr. Carter said: "It'll look even better when it's had its second coat. Just as well the Head put the place out of bounds. Robinson wouldn't be too pleased if his handiwork was spoiled by finger marks all over the wet paint."

"I should think not indeed," Mr. Wilkins replied.

His voice sounded unpleasantly close to the crouchers

within the cubicle. And a moment later they heard him exclaim in surprise: "I say, there's a pair of spectacles down here on the floor, Carter. What on earth are they doing here?"

"Some boy must have left them behind the last time they came in," his colleague replied. "You'd better hand them over to Matron—she'll know whom they belong to."

"Yes, I will . . ." There was a pause while Mr. Wilkins slipped the glasses into his pocket. Then he went on: "I think I'll just take a look inside one of the cubicles. I'd like to see how they look in their new colours."

Jennings and Atkinson froze with horror. Darbishire had been frozen ever since leaving the water some minutes before; but even he experienced a further chilling sensation, as Mr. Wilkins' voice sounded nearer, and his footsteps halted just outside the door of their hiding-place.

CHAPTER 13

DECORATIONS IN THE DARK

MR. WILKINS raised his hand to throw open the cubicle door; another second and the three crouchers would certainly have been discovered. But at the same moment, Mr. Carter's voice rang out warningly from somewhere near the diving board.

"Careful, Wilkins, that paint is still very wet," he said.

His colleague paused, looked hard at the glistening white panels, and slowly dropped his hand to his side.

"So it is: thanks for warning me, Carter. Perhaps it might be better to postpone the inspection for the time being."

He turned and strolled back along the strip of coconut matting which bordered the bath, and shortly afterwards the two masters made their way out of the building, unaware that anything was amiss.

Jennings and Atkinson heaved sighs of relief, while Darbishire, chilled to the marrow, permitted himself the luxury of a long-drawn shiver.

"Phew! I thought we'd had it that time," breathed Atkinson, struggling to free himself from the tightly-packed scrimmage. "Why did you have to leave your glasses on the floor, Darbi? It nearly gave the show away."

"I forgot they were there. I thought I'd got them on," Darbishire explained.

"Surely you could have *seen* you weren't wearing them!"

"No, I couldn't. I can't see very well without my glasses, you see, and . . ."

The pointless argument was interrupted by a sudden wail of dismay, and the two debaters turned to find Jennings pointing at the wall with horrified eyes.

"Petrified paintpots, look what I've done!" he cried.

They followed the direction of his finger, and winced at the sight that met their eyes . . . For near the spot where Jennings was crouching, the gleaming paint was streaked and smeared in a dozen different places. Finger-prints, thumb-prints, hand-prints, and even an elbow-print were plainly visible on what had recently been a smooth, even surface.

It was clear that Jennings was the culprit, for smudges of wet paint were spread over his knuckles, while smaller globules traced a wavering pattern as far as his wrists.

"Fossilised fish-hooks! What a gruesome mess!" cried Atkinson. "However did you come to do that, Jen?"

"I don't know. I've only just seen it," Jennings muttered in worried tones. "Anyway, I couldn't help it. Darbishire was squashing up against me, and I had to lean on something."

"They'll easily find out who's done it," Atkinson prophesied gloomily. "They've only got to photograph the finger-prints and then compare them with——"

"Don't be so stark raving cuckoo, Atki," Jennings retorted irritably. "You'll have them sending for Scotland Yard next. We shall just have to do something about it, that's all."

The situation was indeed grave. Not only had they spoilt the paint, but—and this was far more serious—they had gone into the swimming bath and even entered the water when the building was out of bounds.

Jennings scratched his nose thoughtfully with his sticky white forefinger, while he considered the next move. Obviously the swimming lesson would have to be abandoned, and all their energies concentrated on repairing the damaged paintwork as quickly as possible.

Robinson kept his decorating materials in the tool-shed: Jennings knew that, because only that afternoon he had seen tins of paint, both green and white, stacked just inside the door. One good brushful of white paint should be sufficient to cover the marks he had made. He would do the job at once, before . . .

At that moment the dormitory bell sounded, and Jennings realised that he would have to postpone the work of re-decoration until later in the evening. On no account must they arouse the duty master's suspicions by arriving late in the dormitory.

Darbishire was struck with sudden panic at the sound of the bell.

"Oh, my goodness! Whatever am I going to do!" he wailed, tugging distractedly at his ankles. "I'm all wet and these beastly frogs'-feet won't come off. I can't go flipping into the dormitory in my floppers—er—flapping into the dorm in my flippers."

There was no time, then, to wrestle with the tightly-fitting frogs'-feet; so at Jennings' suggestion, Darbishire slipped into his jacket and shorts and carried his shoes and the rest of his clothes in his hand.

Then the three boys crept out of the swimming bath and hurried in through the side door which led past the boot-lockers to the back stairs. By this means they would avoid the main staircase, and, with any luck, reach their dormitory unobserved.

"Oh, this is gruesome! I wish we'd never done it," Darbishire jerked out through teeth which rattled like a fast-clicking turnstile. "My father says: 'Oh, what a tangled web we weave . . .'"

"Stop moaning, Darbi," Jennings said sharply. "I'm just as badly off as you. Supposing I meet Old Wilkie with ghostly white fingers like the Abominable Snowman."

"Old Wilkie hasn't *got* ghostly white fingers," Darbishire pointed out.

"*My* fingers, you bazooka! If he sees the paint on them, he'll twig in a flash."

This was a matter which might well lead to serious trouble, and they paused near the cloakroom door to consider what could be done about it.

"Couldn't you put some gloves on, or something, till you've had a chance to scrub up a bit?" queried Atkinson. "There's a pair, look, on top of the boot-lockers."

A quick glance was enough to show the weak spot in Atkinson's suggestion.

"But they're boxing gloves!" Jennings protested. "I couldn't get undressed with those things on. I'd never be able to untie my shoe-laces." All the same, they would be better than nothing, he reasoned, for at least they would serve to cover up his hands. With some misgiving he put them on.

The party were low in spirit as they made their way up the back stairs, and most of the blame for their misfortunes was laid at Darbishire's door.

"Ssh, Darbishire! Ssh! Don't flap your feet down so loudly," Jennings hissed in a stage whisper.

"It's these floundering frogs'-feet. They make floppy noises on the lino," Darbishire defended himself.

"Can't you walk on tip-toe, or something?"

"Huh! I'd like to see *you* walking on tip-toe in flippy rubber floppers a foot long!"

"Well, don't slap them down so hard. Every time you go up a couple of steps it sounds like a round of applause."

"If you ask me, the whole thing's old Darbi's fault: pretending he could swim properly when he couldn't all the time—or even *part* of the time," grumbled Atkinson. "I reckon he ought to jolly well do the re-painting by himself."

Jennings nodded in agreement. The task of making good the damage would have to be done later on that evening, for if it was left until the following day, Robinson would be sure to notice it and report the matter to the master on duty.

According to Jennings, the best plan would be for Darbishire to creep down to the tool-shed after silence had been called in the dormitories. Then he could borrow a brush-load of paint, and slip into the swimming bath while the staff were safely out of the way having supper in the dining hall.

The only objections to this scheme came, somewhat naturally, from Darbishire.

"But it'll be dark by then, and I haven't got a torch," he protested. "I haven't even got my glasses. I shan't be able to see what I'm doing."

"You won't *need* to see. You can remember where the paint has got to go, can't you?"

"Well, yes, but . . ."

"Paint it from memory, then. Lots of artists paint from memory; quite decent ones, too—Royal Academy chaps, and all that mob," Jennings said persuasively. "Just get a good brushful of white paint and slap it on the part you squashed me up against."

Darbishire sighed: he was outnumbered and he knew it.

"Oh, all right," he muttered with a bad grace. "But why do these gruesome hoo-hahs always have to pick on *me* to happen to—that's what I want to know!"

When they reached their dormitory they found, to their relief, that Mr. Wilkins was not in the room; though their joy was short-lived when Venables told them that the duty master had commented upon their absence, and was expected to return at any moment.

"Creating like blinko, he was. He said you'd jolly well better be in bed when he came back—or else!" he informed them with relish.

Hastily, Darbishire peeled off his jacket, dabbed his still wet chest and shoulders with his towel, and made a dive for his pyjamas. He was about to tackle the problem of the tight-fitting frogs'-feet when he heard the master returning and jumped into bed without further delay.

Mr. Wilkins was surprised to find Darbishire had undressed so quickly. Then he glanced at the foot of the bed and saw the jacket and shorts lying in an untidy heap on the floor.

"You haven't put your clothes away, Darbishire. Get out of bed and fold them up tidily," he ordered.

Darbishire clutched the sheets tightly around him. "Get out of bed, sir?" he echoed in troubled tones.

"That's what I said. Hurry up, now; I've no time to waste while you . . ."

Mr. Wilkins broke off and stared in amazement as the boy reluctantly pushed back the bedclothes and first one, and then another, green rubber swimming-flipper was revealed against the white background of the sheet.

"I—I—I—— What on earth are those, boy?"

Darbishire looked down at his feet as though unaware that there was anything unusual about them.

"*These*, sir? Oh, these are frogs'-feet, sir! You—er—you swim in them, sir."

"Yes, yes, yes; I know that, you silly little boy. But why in the name of reason do you want to wear the things in bed?"

Darbishire gave a little nervous laugh. "Why, how stupid of me! I must have forgotten to take them off," he said.

"*Doh!*" Mr. Wilkins closed his eyes, clasped his hand to his forehead, and tottered round in small circles. After revolving twice he opened his eyes . . . and saw Jennings standing by the wash-basins trying to undo his shirt buttons with his hands encased in boxing gloves.

"Of all the trumpery moonshine!" Mr. Wilkins exploded. "What do you think you're playing at, Jennings!"

"I was just going to wash my hands, sir."

"What—with *boxing gloves* on!"

The master's voice rose to a squeak of unbelieving protest. The boys must be out of their minds, he thought. Civilised people didn't go to bed in swimming-flippers and boxing gloves. What was the point of affecting such odd slumber-wear? Why, they'd be coming into class in top hats and kilts, if this fantastic behaviour wasn't nipped in the bud!

Jennings started to explain.

"Well, you see, sir, what happened was—well, actually it's rather a long story sir."

But Mr. Wilkins' patience was exhausted, and he had no wish to tax his baffled brain still further by trying to piece together some incredible story that almost certainly wouldn't make sense when it was finished.

"I've no time for long stories when I'm waiting to call silence," he barked. "And I've no time for ridiculous dressing-up games, either. Take those absurd contraptions off your hands and feet, both of you . . . And if you aren't in bed when I come back in two minutes from now, I'll—I'll—well, you'd better *be* in bed in two minutes from now."

He stormed his way out of the room and on to the landing, his mind reeling with the senselessness of it all. There seemed no logical reason for such preposterous behaviour, unless . . . *Unless* it was all part of the elaborate leg-pull which he had first suspected the previous week! . . . Mr. Wilkins halted in mid-stride, trying to fit together the pieces of the puzzle.

First, there had been the extremely courteous conduct and the tender concern for his health; then, some mystery about poking heads into cupboards: and now, this ridiculous exploit which involved retiring to rest in frogs'-feet and boxing gloves. What did it all mean?

Mr. Wilkins brooded over the riddle for some moments, and finally gave it up, as there seemed to be no answer. He felt—as Darbishire had felt some five minutes earlier—that fate was not playing the game in singling him out for more than his fair share of trouble.

"Why do these fantastic things always have to happen when *I'm* on duty?" he asked himself bitterly, as he marched off to call silence in the dormitories.

It was almost dark when Darbishire slipped out of bed and tip-toed down the back stairs on his way to make good the damaged paintwork in the swimming bath.

He was feeling extremely nervous, for such dangerous missions were not at all to his liking; but he gritted his teeth and pressed on, determined not to fail in the task that lay before him.

Much to his surprise, everything went far more smoothly than he had dared to hope. He met no one on the staircase; though when he arrived on the ground floor, a light shining from underneath the dining-hall door gave him an uncomfortable ten seconds as he crept past and out through the side door leading to the quad.

He reached the tool shed in safety, and found the tins of paint and a brush exactly as Jennings had described. There was no time to be lost. Hastily he seized the brush, dipped it into the nearest tin, and then scurried round the corner into the swimming bath, where he stroked the bristles up, down, and across the damaged area of paint.

There was not enough light for him to see his handiwork with a critical eye, but he felt sure that a mixture of memory and guesswork would serve his purpose well enough.

Four minutes later he was back in the dormitory where Jennings was waiting to hear details of the operation.

"How did you get on?" his friend asked, anxiously.

"Oh, famously, thanks—even without my glasses," Darbishire burbled, in a warm glow of triumph and relief. "It was quite easy—in fact, I couldn't help laughing on my way back as I passed the dining-hall."

"Golly! That was risky. They might have heard you."

"Laughing to *myself*, I mean—to think Old Wilkie was inside and didn't know I was creeping past the door. Mind you it was too dark to see properly, so I had to feel my way about and work from memory as you told me; but I'm pretty sure I made a decent job of it. I bet no one will ever guess we had an accident in there."

"We'll beetle downstairs first thing to-morrow and have a look," Jennings decided.

They were awake and dressed some minutes before the rising bell sounded the next morning. Tense with excitement they hurried downstairs and into the swimming bath.

"Funny how it all turned out easier than I'd expected,"

Darbishire was saying as Jennings gingerly opened the cubicle door. "Actually, it was a jolly sight . . . *Glumph!*"

He broke off with a gulp of amazement and stood staring at the cubicle wall with a look of horror in his mild blue eyes . . . For all across the area of his handiwork the white wall was daubed with a layer of bright green paint.

"Fossilised fish-hooks! Whatever have you done?" cried Jennings aghast.

The answer was only too obvious.

"I—I must have dipped the brush in the wrong tin," Darbishire quavered miserably. "There were two tins together, you see, and . . ."

"Yes, but surely you could have seen which was which when you sploshed it on the wall!"

"No, I couldn't. I hadn't got my glasses; and anyway, it was too dark to see properly."

"Don't make feeble excuses. If it was dark anyway. I can't see what you wanted your glasses for."

Jennings was furious at the disastrous outcome of his plan, and he turned on his friend with some heat.

"Honestly, Darbi, I've met some bat-witted clodpolls in my time, but I reckon you win the silver challenge cup for addle-pated beetle-headedness, against all comers!"

And, indeed, there was some cause for his outburst, for the white paint had been so generously re-touched with green, that it looked fifty times worse than the smears and smudges which they had hoped to conceal. There was no possibility now, Jennings pointed out, that such a grave error would go undetected, for Robinson was bound to notice it as soon as he came in to start work.

"There's only one thing to do," he decided at length. "We'll have to go and find Old Robo, and ask him to put it right for us."

"But he always reports things like that; he's never on *our* side," Darbishire objected with some truth; for everyone knew that the odd-job man had little sympathy with boys who wasted his time and impeded his work.

"Yes, I know, but it's our only chance. Perhaps if

we're specially decent to him he may see things in a different light," Jennings observed.

Darbishire uttered a little moan. "Don't talk to me about seeing things in different lights," he said bitterly. "If only there had been *more* light last night, we shouldn't be seeing things so differently now."

He picked up the paint brush which he had absent-mindedly left overnight on the coconut matting beside the bath. Then he followed Jennings out of the building in search of the odd-job man.

They found Robinson in the tool shed, and to their dismay they sensed that his mood was surly, and that he was by no means pleased to see them.

"Good morning, Robinson," said Jennings politely.

"It's not a good morning at all," grumbled the odd-jobber. "All that second coat waiting to be put on the swimming bath, and now I can't even get started."

"Why not?"

"Lost me brush—that's why not. It was here last night on top of this tin of green paint, and now it's gone."

With a guilty start Darbishire realised he was holding the missing article in his hand. How careless of him not to have returned it the previous evening! He was about to restore the property to its rightful owner, when he caught a look from Jennings that warned him to be silent.

"We just looked in to see you, Robinson, to ask if you would very kindly do us a favour," Jennings began.

"I'm always doing you lads favours," came the ungracious reply. "Time somebody did *me* one for a change."

"Of course we will," Jennings answered readily.

Robinson looked at him without enthusiasm. "And what sort of favour do you think you could do for me?"

"We could—er—well, we could try and find your brush for you. That'd be jolly helpful wouldn't it?"

"You'll have a job to find it. Looked everywhere, I have."

"Just you leave it to us," Jennings assured him, "and if we find it, you *will* do us that favour in exchange, won't you?"

"Why! Here's the brush," cried Jennings

"Time to talk about that when you've found it," mumbled Robinson. He moved away to resume his search in a far corner of the shed, and Jennings seized the opportunity to whisper instructions in Darbishire's ear.

"Slip it on that shelf behind the tools," he said quietly. "We mustn't find it too quicly, because he won't be so keen to help us if he knows it was our fault he's lost it."

For some moments they searched with zest. Then Jennings uttered a cry of triumph.

"Why! Here it is," he announced brightly, picking up the brush from the bench where Darbishire had placed it.

Robinson looked surprised. "That's funny; I looked all round there only a few minutes ago. However, did I come to miss seeing it right in front of my nose. Sharp eyes you lads have got!"

The two boys smiled modestly, and Jennings said in his most persuasive tones: "Well, now we've found it for you, you *will* do us that favour, won't you?"

Robinson wasn't very pleased when he heard what the favour was. But he was a man of his word, and at last he agreed to carry out his side of the bargain.

"Whew! What a relief," sighed Jennings, as they watched the odd-jobber plodding off to start his day's work in the swimming bath. "That's got everything nicely settled at last, thank goodness."

"Huh! Don't you believe it," Darbishire muttered. "I've still got to swim in the relay on Friday, don't forget . . . And what's more, I haven't practised going out of my depth, even now!"

CHAPTER 14

RING OUT, WILD BELLS

THE WEEK had started badly for Jennings and Darbishire. Monday's swimming lesson had ended in chaos and confusion, and Tuesday's dawn had revealed the fiasco of the ill-matching paint. On Wednesday events took a turn for

E

the better, and Jennings was able to take advantage of the half-holiday to go in to Linbury and buy the clock which they had planned to give Mr. Wilkins on Thursday afternoon.

It was, of course, important to make sure that no hint of their secret should come to the ears of the staff. It was not only that grown-ups were known to be unreliable about keeping vital information to themselves; but also because this was a scheme which the boys had thought out, all of their own accord, and they had no wish to be thwarted by any well-meant interference from those of riper years.

"Mr. Carter will be on duty this afternoon," Jennings said to Darbishire, as they discussed the matter while washing for lunch. "I expect he'll give me permission to go to the village right enough, but he may ask what I'm going for."

Darbishire looked thoughtful. "It will have to be a genuine reason, too," he observed, for he possessed a tender conscience. "We can't just say *any* old thing if it's not true—besides, he might find out."

He removed his glasses, and polished the dusty lenses on the turnover of his sock. As he was replacing them, one earpiece came away from the frame and dropped to the floor.

"You've bust your glasses," Jennings informed him, somewhat needlessly.

"Oh, that's nothing. Just a screw missing. It probably dropped out when Old Wilkie picked them up in the swimming bath. I spotted it when Matron gave them back to me yesterday, but I thought I'd better not say anything. I'm going to mend it as soon as I can find a decent chunk of fuse wire, or something."

"You jolly well *won't* mend it. It's just what we need for our excuse," Jennings cried with sudden inspiration.

"Eh?" Darbishire was out of his depth.

"Yes, don't you see? I can tell Mr. Carter quite truthfully that I'm going to the jewellers to get your old headlamps fixed; and then I can buy the clock at the same time."

"Wacko! Nimble scheme!" Darbishire approved as the

lunch bell sounded.

Mr. Carter accepted the excuse with only one comment when he granted Jennings' request to go to the village before tea that afternoon.

"I should have thought Darbishire could have taken them to be repaired himself," he remarked.

Jennings shook his head. "Bit risky, sir! He can't see very well without his glasses, and he might fall into a pothole, or march into a telephone box instead of the jeweller's shop, sir."

Mr. Carter thought it unlikely, but he did not argue the point. After all, there was no reason why Jennings should not go if he wanted to.

The first difficulty arose soon after Jennings reached the little shop in Linbury where *H. Higgins, Jeweller and Silversmith,* carried on his trade.

Mr. Higgins provided a screw for the spectacles for the modest sum of one penny: unfortunately, his clocks were rather more expensive.

"Got a nice one here at twelve guineas," he said, turning to a monstrous marble timepiece on the shelf behind him. "Or there's this eight-day chiming model in a walnut case for fourteen pounds ten."

Jennings' spirits sank. "Haven't you got anything cheaper? I've only got a pound—including postal orders and stamps," he said, placing Darbishire's money-box on the counter.

Mr. Higgins peered down at his customer over the top of his gold-rimmed glasses. "Nothing at that price, I'm afraid. Unless, of course, an alarm clock is any use to you?"

Jennings' spirits rose again. An alarm clock would be the very thing!

"May I see one, please," he said.

From under the counter the jeweller produced a shiny green alarm clock with a little knob on the top.

"How about this?" he suggested. "Lovely tick it's got. Good alarm, too: makes enough noise to wake the dead."

He set the clock down on the counter rather more heavily than he had intended, and immediately the alarm went off so loudly that Mr. Higgins jumped in startled surprise.

"Tut-tut-tut. You want to be careful about that," he warned his customer. "A slight jolt on the alarm-winder and up goes the silencer-button, and she's off in a jiffy. Very delicate mechanism these clocks have—very delicate indeed."

Jennings beamed. Did it cost more than a pound, he wanted to know?

Mr. Higgins pursed his lips, and eyed the money-box as though making a great decision. "It should be a guinea, but I'll take a pound, if it's all you've got," he agreed at length.

"Coo, thanks! I'll have it then, please."

Jennings walked back to school clutching the sensitive parcel with extreme care. He felt sure that Mr. Wilkins would be delighted with such a valuable gift. The subscribers, too, would be overjoyed with the way things had been managed on their behalf. One way and another, it seemed that Mr. Wilkins' last lesson with Form 3 would be a time of rejoicing for all concerned.

It was a thousand pities, therefore, that the happy ceremony to which they were looking forward so eagerly should end in unbelievable disaster.

Shortly before afternoon school on Thursday, Jennings marched solemnly into Classroom 3 holding the clock proudly before him, as though bearing an historical emblem in a royal procession. A few of the boys who had not yet seen the farewell gift came crowding round to make sure that their money had been well spent.

They were more than satisfied; and when they heard the nerve-shattering, ear-splitting shrilling of the alarm-bell they plugged their ears with their fingers and leaped up and down in ecstasies of delight.

"Wacko! Isn't it super!" Venables shouted about the jangling uproar. "This ought to wake him up all right when he gets to this new school he's going to."

"It goes on for ever so long if you let it," Jennings explained, switching off the alarm and setting it again at random. "I vote we put it in the cupboard till the end of the lesson. Then we'll dish it out, while old Darbi gets cracking on his famous speech."

Darbishire looked up importantly from a sheaf of notes on his desk.

"That's right," he said. "I've learnt it all off by heart. Would you like to hear how it goes?"

"No, I wouldn't," said Jennings shortly, as he slipped the clock into the cupboard and closed the door with a slam.

"Well, I'll tell you then," Darbishire went on unabashed. "As soon as the lesson's over, I'm going to stand up and say—'Mr. Wilkins and Gentlemen: Unaccustomed as I am to public speaking, it gives me great pleasure to be very happy to come here this afternoon, which reminds me of a quotation from *Julius Cæsar*, Book One . . .'"

"Look out, he's coming," hissed Temple, who was keeping watch at the classroom door.

The boys scurried to their desks, pleased and proud at the thought of all the pleasure which their generous gift would soon be bringing to Mr. Wilkins.

The only sound in the room now came from Darbishire, practising his speech for the last time in a voiceless whisper . . . "Mr. Wilkins and Gentlemen: Unaccustomed as I am . . ."

The door swung open . . . L. P. Wilkins, Esq., M.A. (Cantab.), had arrived for what was generally believed to be his last lesson with Form 3.

The master was slightly taken aback by the unusual silence; he was aware, too, that the atmosphere was tense and expectant.

Obviously something was afoot! . . . Mr. Wilkins frowned. Just let them try any funny business, he thought —just let them *try*, that's all! His disapproving stare swivelled round and came to rest on Darbishire.

"What were you saying just then, when I came in?" he demanded.

Darbishire gave him a disarming smile.

"I was just saying, unaccustomed as I was, sir."

"Unaccustomed as you were to *what*?"

"Oh, nothing, really, sir. It doesn't matter." Darbishire smiled again. It would not do to reveal the secret before the proper moment arrived . . . Mr. Wilkins would know soon enough!

Bristling with suspicion, Mr. Wilkins strode to the master's desk and opened a copy of Tennyson's *In Memoriam*.

"Now, first of all, I'm going to read you some verses by Alfred, Lord Tennyson, and then I'm going to ask you some questions about them," he announced. "So all sit up straight and keep your wits about you."

He cleared his throat, and spoke in the special dramatic tones which he always used when reading poetry aloud to the form.

"Ring Out, Wild Bells," by Alfred, Lord Tennyson:

> " 'Ring out, wild bells, to the wild sky,
> *The flying cloud, the frosty light:*
> *The year is dying in the night;*
> *Ring out, wild bells, and . . .' "*

Temple put up his hand.

"Put your hand down, boy. I will *not* be interrupted when I'm reading," barked Mr. Wilkins.

"Sorry, sir. I only wondered whether you meant we should have to write the questions in our books, sir."

"Of *course* you'll write them in your books. You don't imagine I want them carved on a marble slab do you? Now, no more silly interruptions.

> " 'Ring out, wild bells, to the wild sky,
> *The flying cloud, the frosty light:*
> *The year . . .' "*

A shattering burst of coughing, like a fusillade of machine-gun fire, drowned his next words. Venables, the unintentional culprit, hastened to express his deep regret.

"Sorry, sir. It's my cough, sir. Matron's very kindly giving me some medicine for it, but . . ."

"All right, all *right*! Only keep it quiet while I'm reciting." He started again:

" 'Ring out, wild bells, to the wild sky . . .' "

There came a knocking at the door. Mr. Wilkins paused, and then decided to ignore the interruption.

" 'Ring out, wild bells, to the . . .' "

The knocking was repeated, louder this time, as though the visitor had brought a steam-hammer with him to reinforce his efforts.

Angry, now, Mr. Wilkins abandoned his recital of the works of Alfred, Lord Tennyson, and shouted: "Oh, come in! . . . Come in for goodness' sake! Don't stand out there performing percussion band solos on the door. Come *in*, if you must! "

The door opened to admit Atkinson, arriving late for class owing to the mysterious disappearance of a pair of house shoes.

"Sorry I'm late, sir," he apologised breezily. "I couldn't find my shoes, sir."

"You should have been here five minutes ago," fumed Mr. Wilkins.

"Why? What happened, sir? Did I miss something?"

"Doh!" Mr. Wilkins thumped the works of Alfred, Lord Tennyson, in exasperation. "I mean you were late for my lesson. This is the third time I've tried to recite this poem without getting beyond the first few lines, and if I hear one more sound from this class I'll—I'll—well, there had better not *be* one more sound! "

It was becoming evident to Form 3 that the happy atmosphere so necessary for the presentation of farewell gifts was sadly lacking. They sat still as statues, determined that Mr. Wilkins should have no further cause to complain. So still were they that the dropping of a pin would have been clearly audible, and after a few seconds the master decided to try again.

"Ring Out, Wild Bells, by Alfred, Lord Tennyson," he announced dramatically. He cleared his throat and began:

" 'Ring out, wild bells . . .' "

He got no further . . . For at that instant the peaceful atmosphere was shattered by the ear-splitting, nerve-rending shrilling of a bell from within the cupboard.

It was a harsh, jarring scream of a noise, which, in the quiet classroom, sounded as loud as the whistle of a locomotive, the blare of a ship's siren and the whine of a jet aircraft engine all rolled into one vast pandemonium of sound.

Mr. Wilkins leaped like a mountain goat. The volume of verse shot from his nerveless fingers and described a somersault in mid-air before landing face downwards on a desk in the front row . . . And all the time the shrilling of the alarm bell went on . . . and on . . . and on.

Form 3 sat numb with hopeless despair while their form-master sought to regain control of his outraged feelings. At last he found his voice.

"I—I—! Who's ringing out that wild bell? . . . I mean, who's responsible for . . . for this disgraceful behaviour?"

The alarm ran down and the ringing ceased as Jennings raised his hand.

"It wasn't meant to go off then, sir. It was just a terrible accident," he explained in a distressed voice. "It was a special secret surprise that we were planning for you, sir."

"How dare you plan secret surprises in my lesson? I never heard of such a thing. Insolence . . . impudence . . . impertinence. And this, I suppose, is the real meaning of all the outrageous conduct I've noticed lately!"

"Oh, no, sir!"

"Oh, *yes*, sir! You were planning this ridiculous trick of letting off wild alarm bells in the middle of my lesson!"

"But, sir, you don't understand, sir."

But Mr. Wilkins was convinced that at last he *did* understand, and that he had solved the mystery that had been worrying him for the last ten days.

It seemed clear to him, now, that the displays of politeness, the concern for his health, the poking of heads into cupboards—even the frogs'-feet and boxing gloves—were connected in some subtle way with the absurd joke of which he had just been made the victim . . . Very well, then! *He* would show them he wasn't the sort of man to be trifled with!

"Take that thing—whatever it is—out of the cupboard, and bring it up to me at once!" he thundered.

Heavy in heart, Jennings obeyed ... If only Mr. Wilkins would listen! If only he would give them a chance to explain!

But Mr. Wilkins wouldn't listen. His dignity had suffered and he was extremely annoyed. As the presentation clock was laid on the desk before him, he burst out angrily: "How you had the audacity, Jennings, to hide this thing in the cupboard, and set it off in the middle of my lesson, I—I—well, I don't know!"

"Oh, but, sir, I didn't, sir. It's very sensitive you see, sir," Jennings faltered when the master paused for breath.

"Quiet, boy! I shall confiscate this—this monstrous contraption," Mr. Wilkins announced, placing the clock inside the master's desk. "And, furthermore, I shall report this form to the headmaster for insolent and impertinent behaviour. . . . And now we will proceed with the lesson."

He glared at the rows of unhappy faces before him, and then picked up his book of poems.

" ' Ring out, wild bells, to the wild sky,
    The flying cloud, the frosty night ...' "

His voice boomed on, but Form 3 were too stunned by the disaster to pay any attention to his words. Their hopes and plans, the happy atmosphere and the joy of giving—all these lay in ruins.

But how could it be otherwise when people were so tactless as to confiscate their own farewell gifts!

An emergency meeting of all subscribers to the *Mr.-Wilkins'-Farewell-Gift-Fund* was held in the Common Room that evening. The proceedings were somewhat informal, and most of the time was spent in shouting down the unfortunate Chairman, whenever he tried to make himself heard above the general uproar.

"It's all your fault anyway, Jennings," proclaimed Venables wrathfully. "If you hadn't let the clock go off while Old Wilkie was woffling about ringing out wild bells, we shouldn't be up a gum-tree now."

"I couldn't help it. How was I to know what he was going to woffle about?" Jennings protested. "It was just a ghastly accident that it went off like that. The chap in the shop said the works were a bit touchy."

Thinking back, he could see how the trouble had occurred: when he had re-set the alarm at random, after his demonstration, he must have left it timed to go off some minutes after the lesson had started. Even so, all would have been well, had not the slamming of the cupboard door jerked the silencer-button from its rest and left the bell ready to jangle into action when the fateful moment arrived.

"Well, it's no good moaning about whose fault it was," Martin-Jones pointed out reasonably. "The important thing is, what are we going to do now?"

It was a thorny problem, for whichever way they looked at it they kept coming back to the unanswerable question: how was it possible to give a present to someone who had already taken it by force?

Brows were knitted and foreheads were furrowed as they sought for some way out of the difficulty.

"What makes it a jolly sight worse is that Old Wilkie doesn't even know that it's his *own* property he's confiscated," Atkinson observed gloomily.

Bromwich was the only subscriber who refused to view the unexpected turn of events with concern. He had not witnessed the afternoon's fiasco in the classroom, for at the time he had been in the sick room recovering from the cold in the head which had caused him to be listed as a doubtful starter for the swimming relay the following day. At tea-time, however, Matron had allowed him to go downstairs, where he soon learned of the recent tragic developments.

"I can't see why you're kicking up such a hoo-hah about it," he remarked during a lull in the debate. "After all, you *wanted* Old Wilkie to have the clock, didn't you?"

"Yes, of course we did."

"Well, now he's *got* it, hasn't he! So what are you all moaning about?"

"Ah, but we wanted to *give* it to him. We didn't want him to take it without even knowing what it was," Darbishire observed. "And then, there's my speech, too. I spent hours learning it off by heart; all about how happy I was, and what pleasure it gave me on this important occasion . . ."

"Well, it wouldn't have given *us* any pleasure," retorted Temple curtly. "The only nimble thing about the whole frantic issue is that we didn't have to sit and listen to you woffing your head off about how happy you were."

The discussion rambled on, and most of the argument was so far from the point that Jennings was in despair of finding a solution to the problem. Time was short: early the following morning Mr. Wilkins would be leaving for his new school, his mind filled with bitter thoughts of Form 3, instead of the pleasant memories they had tried so hard to invoke.

Something drastic would have to be done, Jennings decided; so leaving the embittered wranglers to argue amongst themselves, he slipped out of the Common Room and went off to find Mr. Carter, determined to ask his advice.

Mr. Carter was marking books in his study when Jennings' woebegone features appeared round the door.

"Sir, please, sir, may I speak to you? Something terrible has happened, sir," the boy began.

"I'm sorry to hear it. Anything I can do to put matters right?" asked Mr. Carter, laying down his pen.

Jennings was uncertain how to embark on his tale of woe. "Well, sir, it's like this. We all clubbed together and bought Mr. Wilkins an alarm clock, sir."

Mr. Carter looked puzzled. "Very generous of you, Jennings, but why?"

"We thought he'd like it, sir. We were going to give it to him at the end of the lesson, and Darbishire had prepared a famous speech, but the alarm went off in the middle . . ."

"In the middle of the speech?"

"No, in the middle of the lesson, sir. And Mr. Wilkins

thought we were trying to be funny, and he confiscated it, sir. And now all the chaps are asking how we can give him his present when he's got it already, but doesn't know, sir."

Mr. Carter agreed that the circumstances were most unfortunate. At the same time he could not quite understand

what was behind it all. What, he inquired, had prompted this unusual display of generosity?

"Well, sir," Jennings explained, "as soon as we heard he was leaving, we decided to . . ."

"*Leaving?*"

Mr. Carter sat bolt upright in his chair and his eyebrows rose in surprise. "What makes you think that Mr. Wilkins is leaving?"

"Everyone knows he is, sir. I heard him telling Matron. He said he was going first thing to-morrow morning, sir."

Mr. Carter shook his head sadly, and "tut-tutted" in patient rebuke.

"What a pity you didn't make sure of your facts, Jennings," he said quietly. "Mr. Wilkins is certainly leaving to-morrow morning . . . *But he's coming back on Monday.* He's only going away for the week-end."

"What!"

The room swam before Jennings' eyes, and he goggled at Mr. Carter in speechless amazement . . . Mr. Wilkins coming back! So they needn't have bought the farewell gift after all . . . Fossilised fish-hooks! What on earth would all the subscribers say, he wondered. They would feel cheated: perhaps they would demand their money back—an impossible request, seeing that it had all been spent and the proceeds confiscated.

"Oh, sir, what a ghastly catastroscope," the boy stammered at length. "Of course, I'm glad he's really coming back, but I was just thinking . . ." He tailed off into silence. How could he put his feelings into words at a time like this?

Mr. Carter noticed his look of anguish, and said: "You seem to have got things in a bit of a tangle, Jennings. I think perhaps I'd better see Mr. Wilkins for you, and try to straighten out the—er—little misunderstanding."

"Oh, sir, would you really, sir?"

Mr. Carter nodded. It might be as well, he thought, not to disturb his colleague on the eve of his departure, when he would be busy packing. The new suit had arrived just in time; and at that moment Mr. Wilkins would probably be admiring his reflection in the mirror, and in no mood to listen to long-winded explanations from Form 3.

"I can't see him to-night because he's busy," Mr. Carter said, "but I think you can safely look forward to having your property restored when he comes back on Monday."

"Thank you ever so much, sir."

Jennings felt a little better at the thought that Mr. Carter was willing to act as a go-between; but even so he tottered from the study in a daze of dejection and despair. Whatever was he going to do? How could he face the already

141

indignant subscribers and tell them that their hard-won threepences had been squandered to no purpose?

Besides, supposing Mr. Wilkins *did* give the clock back, what on earth would they do with the wretched timepiece then? Whichever way one looked at it, the whole sorry business ranked as one of the most tragic disasters of modern times.

In the dormitory that evening, Jennings did his best to break the tidings gently.

"I say, you chaps; I've got some supersonic news for you," he announced with a forced smile. "We needn't worry about not being able to give Old Wilkie his clock, because he won't be needing it after all."

"Why not?" demanded Dormitory 6 suspiciously.

"Because—well, because he's not leaving."

The subscribers were thunderstruck by this sensational announcement.

"Old Wilkie not leaving?" echoed Temple. "But you gruesome specimen, Jennings, it was you who told us that he *was*!"

"Yes, I know. I made a bit of a bish about that," Jennings confessed. "But Mr. Carter's going to see him and straighten everything out for us."

"What about our contributions?" stormed Temple. "I gave a whole threepence, I'll have you remember."

"So did I. False pretences, that's what it is," fumed Atkinson. "You're a bogus swizzler, Jennings, and I jolly well demand my money back."

"Money back?" Jennings looked pained and surprised to think that anyone should bring up such a vulgar topic at a time like this. "Haven't you chaps got any decent feelings at all? Why, you said you were *sorry* when you thought he was leaving. You forked out those threepences to show how upset you were."

"What's that got to do with it?" demanded Temple.

"Well, now he's *not* leaving, you ought to be jolly glad. Dash it all, look at the bargain you're getting for three-pence!"

It was clear from the puzzled expressions of his audience

142

that they did not follow Jennings' line of reasoning. He tried to put it more plainly.

"Well, it's like an insurance policy, really. You pay your threepences, and that guarantees that Old Wilkie stays on."

Atkinson still felt that there was a flaw in this argument somewhere, but as he could not be bothered to work it out he hurried on to the next point that occurred to him.

"Yes, but look here, what about the clock?" he demanded. "If Old Wilkie's not having it, what are we going to do with the thing?"

"Just leave that to me," said Jennings with a conviction he was far from feeling. "Everything'll be all right you see!"

"It had *better* be," threatened Temple. "I'm not having my threepence wasted, or there'll be some bashing-up going on around these parts. You mark my words!"

Jennings gave him a disarming smile. "Trust me: I won't let you down."

He spoke with a quiet confidence that did much to calm their fears, and the little group of subscribers wandered off to the washbasins wondering whether, perhaps, they had not been rather hasty in condemning the action of their Chairman before he had had a chance to straighten things out.

According to Jennings, there was nothing to worry about. Very well then, they reasoned, let him put matters right in his own way—and good luck to him!

They clambered into bed feeling assured that Jennings had the matter well in hand; though it is doubtful if they would have felt so easy in their minds, had they guessed that he had not the slightest idea of how he was going to solve this latest, pressing problem.

CHAPTER 15

DARBISHIRE TAKES THE PLUNGE

OF THE seventy-nine boarders of Linbury Court School who awoke the next morning to the sound of the rising bell, only one failed to leap from his bed tingling with a thrill of anticipation . . .

It was Friday, the day of the inter-house junior swimming relay, for which they had been practising so long. And as if this was not enough to rejoice all hearts, there was the added pleasure of knowing that they would escape the usual Friday maths test, for Mr. Wilkins was even then preparing to depart for London by the first train after breakfast.

But the seventy-ninth boarder was C. E. J. Darbishire, and the excited atmosphere aroused no answering echo in his heart. He sat up in bed surveying the happy revellers with a jaundiced eye, and wishing that he could bury himself beneath the blankets and hibernate until the junior relay was safely over. The senior boys in *Drake* had already played their part in bringing honour to their House. Now, it was up to the younger ones to show what they could do.

"What are you looking so fossilised about, Darbi?" Atkinson asked, weaving his head through the neck of his shirt. "You look about as cheerful as a corncrake with chilblains."

"Surely you haven't forgotten," groaned Darbishire with a slight shudder. "I've got to swim the first lap for *Drake;* and thanks to old Jennings bishing up the issue the other evening, I haven't tried going out of my depth yet."

"Oh, no: so you haven't!"

So much had happened since the ill-fated swimming

lesson, that Atkinson had hardly given a second thought to Darbishire's plight. In any case, he reasoned, it was not really his business, for when he had been asked to help in the scheme, he had agreed only to act as a sentry outside the door, and what had happened after *that*, he preferred to forget!

"Oh, you'll be all right," Atkinson consoled him. "Just keep on till you can't swim any longer. With any luck you'll be somewhere near the shallow end by then, so you'll be able to put your foot down and take a breather."

"All very well to talk about breathers in the shallow end," lamented Darbishire. "I've got to get there first, and that means kicking off in deep water."

"What of it? There'll be masses of chaps ready to jump in and lug you out, if you turn turtle and founder with all hands."

Atkinson did his best to sound sympathetic, but his voice betrayed the fact that he was agog with curiosity to know what would happen when the great moment arrived. Apart from Jennings and Darbishire, he was the only boy in the school who knew of the predicament in which the *Drake* junior team was placed.

According to Jennings, it was vital that the awkward secret should not be allowed to leak out, if only for the sake of keeping up morale. Besides, he had argued, it was quite likely that Darbishire would be able to make the grade if only he set his mind to it.

Atkinson wasn't so sure! He felt he *ought* to be sorry for Darbishire, but unfortunately this was out of the question. For Atkinson was a member of the opposing House of *Raleigh*.

"Well, cheer up anyway, Darbi. Whatever happens it ought to be well worth watching," he remarked as he turned away towards the wash-basins.

Darbishire shuddered at the thought of the ordeal before him. Why, oh why, he asked himself, had he ever been so stark raving mad as to pretend he was an accomplished swimmer, when in point of fact a few floundering strokes was all he could manage without using one leg as a punt-pole!

145

Perhaps, even now, it would not be too late to go to Mr. Carter and confess: but even as he toyed with the idea he knew he would never be able to live down the curt comments and derisive laughter of his colleagues. Besides, he would *have* to swim for his House: with Bromwich listed as a non-starter, there was no other novice qualified to take part in the lap limited to beginners.

All through the first two lessons Darbishire sat in a trance of anxiety, and on several occasions Mr. Carter took him to task for not paying attention. At mid-morning break he wandered out on to the quad, but took no part in the babble of small-talk raging round the great event of the day.

"I reckon *Raleigh* will win the junior by about 100 miles," prophesied Binns. "Well, two or three feet anyway."

"Don't be such a lobsterous clodpoll," countered Blotwell. "*Drake's* bound to win. We've got Darbishire for the first lap, don't forget. He goes belting along like a torpedo going *slap-bang-whoosh* through the sound barrier."

Darbishire overheard this fragment of praise, and felt even worse than before.

"You should just see his revolving, cork-screw paddle-steamer stroke, with jet propelled ankle movements," Blotwell went on. "He was saying only last week that he may even be asked to demonstrate it on television in the holidays."

Binns was impressed. Clearly, *Raleigh* had no swimmer who could make much of a showing against such an outstanding performer. Loyally he said: "Well, anyway, we've got Thompson swimming against him in the first lap, and he's not at all bad, really."

"Thompson!" snorted Blotwell contemptuously. "Why, a feeble specimen like old Thompo doesn't stand an earthly against a human fish like Darbishire."

The human fish sidled away out of earshot, pink to the ears with embarrassment.

On the far side of the quad he saw Bromwich frisking up and down with the energy of a charging buffalo, and looking extremely robust for one still on the sick list. It was most unfair, thought Darbishire, that old Bromo should be classed as a delicate invalid unable to swim for his House, when he was obviously bursting with rude health. What on earth was Matron thinking of to let herself be hoodwinked in this shameless manner!

Jennings came trotting up at that moment. "How are you feeling?" he asked breezily.

Darbishire forced a wan smile.

"Mouldy! I've got the heeby-jeebies." he said with a dry swallow.

"Don't talk such gruesome eye-wash. You'll be all right when once you get started. After all, you *can* swim—just about!"

"It's the starting-off bit that gets me down," Darbishire confessed. "It looks about as deep as Mount Everest the other way up, if you know what I mean."

"Well, start off with a supersonic jump, and that'll take you quite a bit of the way," Jennings said airily. "Martin-Jones and I will be at the opposite end waiting for you and old Petters, so we'll be able to cheer you on. Everything will be all right when you get started, you see. You may even enjoy it!"

After break, Darbishire became a little more cheerful. Perhaps it wouldn't be so bad after all! He would swim close in to the side, within reach of the hand-rail, he decided. He knew he would be all right for the first five or six strokes; perhaps, with a special effort, he could manage seven, or even eight, and by that time *surely* he would be approaching the four-foot mark, where he would be able to touch bottom on tip-toe. From there, he could hop the rest of the way, if necessary . . . He'd be all right, he told himself, over and over again. There was nothing to worry about, really!

But at four o'clock that afternoon, when he found himself standing on the edge of the bath waiting for the starter's signal, his easy assurance drained away, and his spirits sank once more to zero.

"All boys in the junior relay teams line up in your places," Mr. Carter announced. "I'm starting the race in half a minute from now."

The swimming teams consisted of four junior boys from each of the two Houses, *Drake* and *Raleigh*. The first and third pairs of rivals swam one length from the deep end to the shallow, while the second and fourth pairs swam their length in the opposite direction.

Owing to Mr. Wilkins' absence, Mr. Hind had been enlisted as a judge. He took up his station at the shallow end, to make sure that the change-overs were fairly carried out; while Mr. Carter undertook similar duties at the deep end where the edge of the bath marked both the start and the finish of the race.

The headmaster, also, had decided to grace the proceedings with his presence, and now stood by the springboard beaming affably in all directions. He held a bath towel before him to save his trousers from being drenched by unskilful divers.

Pettigrew, the third swimmer for *Drake*, took his place by the wall at the deep end. He was a portly youth of twelve, with an untidy mop of fair hair which hung down over his forehead like a fringe on a lamp-shade.

"Wake up, Darbi," he said briskly. "It's you and me starting here, and Martin-J. and Jen at the other end. Try and get a decent lead over Thompson and don't slow down in the last few yards, because Martin isn't allowed to dive off until you actually touch the wall at the far end."

Darbishire gulped. The far end was barely thirty yards away, yet it seemed a distant speck on the horizon in his present state of nervousness.

"Then, when Martin-J. gets back here, I'll take off on the third lap," Pettigrew went on chattily, "and after that it's up to old Jennings to finish off the rest."

A strangled croak, like the cry of an adenoidal bullfrog, forced its way through Darbishire's vocal chords, signifying that he understood what he was expected to do.

He stole a glance at Thompson, his *Raleigh* opponent for the first lap, who was standing beside him. He had an easy, confident air about him, Darbishire thought. But then, so he should: after all, Thompson had swum out of his depth dozens of times.

"Quiet, everybody, for the start of the relay," Mr. Carter ordered; and the spectators lining the walls ceased their chattering and craned forward expectantly.

Thompson and Darbishire stepped towards their marks, and braced themselves for what they hoped would turn out to be a skilful racing dive.

The starter's voice rang out loud and clear: "Take your marks . . ."

At that moment there was a sudden commotion by the door at the entrance to the bath, and Bromwich, clad in bathing-wrap and swimming trunks, came hurrying in past the spectators, shrilling out a message of dire urgency.

"Sir! . . . Sir! . . . Mr. Carter, sir; wait a second. Don't start yet, please, sir!"

Mr. Carter paused in the act of mouthing the word: "Go."

"What's the matter, Bromwich?" he demanded.

"Please, sir, I've just been to see Matron. She says my cold is a lot better, and I can swim after all, sir."

Mr. Carter looked doubtful. "It's a bit late in the day to change the teams, Bromwich. Darbishire's swimming in your place."

"Oh, *please*, sir," Bromwich begged, hopping up and down to stress the urgency of his plea. "I couldn't come earlier because I couldn't find her, sir; but now I'm all changed and ready to go in, and Darbishire's only a reserve after all, sir."

"H'm! Well, if your swimming captain agrees, and the reserve doesn't mind standing down . . ."

"Oh, *he* won't mind, sir," Jennings' voice rang out from the shallow end. "He's not a bit selfish, are you, Darbi?"

A martyr at the stake could not have shown a nobler spirit of self-sacrifice than Darbishire did then.

"That's all right, sir," he said. "I'm a bit disappointed, of course, but I don't mind standing down for the sake of *Drake*."

"Very generous of you, Darbishire," nodded the headmaster approvingly. "I always like to see boys putting their team first, and themselves last."

A few seconds later Bromwich was lined up beside Thompson, and Mr. Carter was preparing to start the race for the second time.

"Take your marks . . . Go!"

There was a loud smack as the swimmers hit the water in a racing dive . . . The junior relay had begun!

Immediately the quiet hush gave place to roars of encouragement as the spectators shouted for *Drake* or *Raleigh*, with the full force of their lungs.

"Go it, Thompson! Swim up! Faster! Faster!"

"Stick it, Bromo! Come on! Try and take the lead!"

It was clear from the outset that the teams were evenly matched, for Bromwich and Thompson propelled their way down the bath without either boy gaining an advantage on the other. The second lap, also, was practically a dead heat, but when the third pair of swimmers launched themselves into the water, Pettigrew began to lose way against his stronger *Raleigh* opponent.

By this time, Darbishire had recovered from the shock of his merciful deliverance, and was cavorting with excitement on the extreme edge of the coconut matting. "Go it, Petters! Go it!" he yelled.

"Budge out of the light, Darbi. I can't see a thing with you dancing about like a hippopotamus right in front of me," complained Atkinson from the second row of spectators.

But Darbishire had no ears for curt complaint, and no eyes for anything but the race. By now, Pettigrew's opponent had reached the end of the bath, and the last *Raleigh* swimmer had dived in on the final lap, while Jennings was still waiting in a frenzy of impatience for his turn to go.

At last Pettigrew touched the wall, and Jennings set off in pursuit of his rival with a splash that sent a tidal wave billowing over the feet of the excited spectators.

"Go it, Jen," Darbishire shouted, as his friend slowly narrowed the gap between him and his rival. "He's gaining! . . . He's catching up! . . . Oh, super-wacko-sonic!"

"Stand back, you boys, stand back," ordered Mr.

Carter, as the spectators surged dangerously towards the edge of the bath.

Gradually Jennings drew level, and the two swimmers raced neck and neck towards the finish, each vainly striving to forge ahead. Soon there were only three yards to go . . . two yards . . .

"Go it, Jen!" yelled Darbishire, hysterical with excitement. "He's going to do it! . . . No, he isn't . . . Yes, he is . . . He's *done* it!"

At the same instant, the *Drake* captain's hand shot out of the water and touched the wall, a bare second ahead of his opponent.

"Hooray! hooray! We've won by a fingernail!" warbled the happy reservist, celebrating the victory with an impromptu ballet on the edge of the bath. "Good old *Drake*! Good old Jennings! Good old . . ."

The spate of congratulations ceased suddenly as the speaker caught his foot on the corner of the coconut matting . . . For a moment he danced upon air like a clumsy puppet, his legs back-pedalling in a frantic effort to regain his balance. The next second there was a resounding splash, as C. E. J. Darbishire plunged head-first into six feet of water.

A roar of laughter swept through the ranks of the spectators as the unwitting diver's head rose to the surface . . . There was no need to worry! After all, a strong swimmer like old Darbi should be able to take an accidental ducking like that in his stride.

But Atkinson knew better.

"Sir! Sir!" he called to Mr. Carter. "Darbishire's gone in out of his depth, sir."

"It won't hurt him—he's got his swimming things on," replied Mr. Carter with a smile.

"Yes, but sir—*he can't swim*! Not out of his depth, anyway!"

"What!"

Mr. Carter did not waste time disputing this surprising statement. He dashed to the side of the bath, ready, if need be, to dive fully-clothed to the rescue.

It was not necessary. As he stood poised to dive, a

triumphant cry rang out from the curly head bobbing about in the water.

"It's all right, sir—don't bother. I've just made a wonderful discovery, sir . . . I *can* swim!"

And indeed this was no boastful exaggeration. After weeks of striving, the knack had come to him suddenly and without warning. And now, for the first time in his life, he found himself swimming out of his depth with an easy confidence.

Bursting with pride, he turned towards the spectators and announced at the top of his voice: "Watch me, everybody: I can swim! . . . I can swim! . . . *I can swim!*"

CHAPTER 16

FAREWELL TO THE GIFT

Mr. WILKINS arrived back in time for school on Monday morning, and with his return the question of how to dispose of the alarm clock became hourly more acute.

During the week-end, the junior swimming relay had been such a raging topic of conversation that no one could be bothered to argue about anything else. But now that things were back to normal, it was agreed on all sides that the problem of the confiscated time-piece ranked as one of the gravest social injustices of the twentieth century.

Mr. Carter did his best to straighten things out. He had a word with Mr. Wilkins during morning break, and as a result the clock was handed back to Jennings without more ado. But far from settling matters, this seemed rather to aggravate the difficulties still further.

"You'll jolly well have to do something about it, and pretty quickly too, Jen," Darbishire said, as the boys were changing in the pavilion after cricket practice that afternoon. "Temple and Atkinson were creating like blinko all through lunch. They reckon they've been swindled, and they jolly well want their share given back to them—or else!"

"What do they expect me to do—bust the clock up into seventy-nine small chunks and give everyone a bit each?"

With an impatient gesture, Jennings turned to his clothes-peg and started to change; and then a brilliant thought struck him and he turned to his friend, his eyes shining with inspiration.

"I know, Darbi; I'll raffle it! I'll go round collecting threepence from everyone as the price of a ticket: then I'll pick a number out of a hat, and the winner gets the clock!"

Darbishire looked at Jennings with a mixture of pity and despair. "You need your head seeing to," he said sorrowfully. "Of all the bat-witted schemes I ever heard, I reckon that one's the battiest."

"I don't see why. If I did that, I should be able to give all the farewell gift subscribers their money back."

"If!—if!—if!" retorted Darbishire impatiently. "Don't you realise there isn't a single character in the whole school who'd fork out so much as a trouser button for another of your hare-brained wheezes? You've got a fat hope if you think they're going to part with another three-pence before they've even got their first one back!"

Jennings sighed. He knew in his heart that Darbishire's curt comment summed up the position in a nutshell: as a floater of financial schemes, the reputation of J. C. T. Jennings was at a low ebb.

"Well, all I can say is, it's a mouldy unfair chizz, and I'm just about fed up with the whole issue," he complained, slipping his belt round his waist. "I go to all the trouble of organising Old Wilkie's leaving present, and then, just because he decides to come back after all, everybody turns on me and says . . . Ow! . . . Ouch! . . . Fossilised fish-hooks!"

He stopped suddenly in the act of reaching for his jacket, as a sharp pain seared into the small of his back and made him catch his breath. He leant forward, hunching his shoulders, and again felt the agonising stab.

"Ow! . . . Ooh! . . . This is chronic," he groaned.

"What's up?" asked Darbishire.

"I don't know. I've got a pain just here." Jennings

153

crooked his elbow to indicate the site of his affliction, and then stopped with a gasp. "Wow! There it is again! Golly, I hope I didn't disconnect my backbone when I dived in for the relay on Friday."

"I expect it's lumbago," said Darbishire solemnly. "Or tennis elbow, perhaps."

"Don't be such a crazy bazooka! You can't catch tennis elbow in swimming baths."

"Well, channel-swimmer's shoulder blade, then—or even gout. I should go and see Matron at once, if I were you. Tell her you've got a pain in your foot."

"But it's nowhere near my foot," the sufferer protested. "It's up here in my . . . Ow!"

"Not if it's gout, it isn't. Must be in your foot, unless it's slipped a bit," Darbishire observed. "My father knew a man once who had housemaid's knee, and all because of . . ."

"Oh, shut up, Darbi," Jennings turned on his friend with some heat. "Here I am in ghastly agony with a warped back-bone, or something, and all you can do is to stand there woffling a lot of gobbledeygook about your father catching housemaid's gout. Dash it all, *I* ought to know where it hurts, considering it's my pain."

Darbishire pursed his lips and stroked an imaginary beard. He felt clear in his mind that he had diagnosed the complaint, but as the case appeared to be bristling with complications it might, perhaps, be better to seek a second opinion.

"Well, just go and tell Matron you're in ghastly agony," he advised.

Jennings was only too willing to go. Matron's sitting-room was the obvious place of refuge for anyone suffering from as many troubles as he had to contend with. Not only would she cure the mysterious pain in his back but, with any luck, she might even be able to solve his other problem and suggest the best way of dealing with angry subscribers to unwanted alarm clocks. Surely a little matter like that should present no difficulty to a fully-qualified Matron.

He limped painfully indoors and made his way up the

stairs. Every now and then he stopped with a gasp as the stabbing pain caught him in the back; but at last he reached the door of Matron's room and tottered across the threshold.

Fortunately she was on duty. She invited him in and inquired the reason for his staggering gait.

"Oh, Matron, I'm suffering terrible tortures, Matron," he lamented. "It started when I changed back after cricket, and Darbishire thinks it's housemaid's elbow."

Matron received the news calmly. She had often encountered Darbishire's medical case-work in the past, and was used to treating chilblains and blisters which he had diagnosed quite positively as frostbite and blood-poisoning.

"Where does it hurt you?" she asked.

"Well, it's all right when I'm standing still, Matron," Jennings explained. "But as soon as I jump about, or try to do hand-stands and things, something seems to bite me in the back. What do you think I ought to do, Matron?"

"I would suggest *not* doing hand-stands," she returned pleasantly. "Slip your jacket off, and I'll have a look."

One glance was enough to reveal the cause of the trouble.

"Yes, I see what it is," she said. "A clear case of twisted-belt-buckle-itis."

"Wow! That sounds bad," Jennings exclaimed. "Shall I have to see the doctor, Matron?"

"Oh, no, it's not serious." She straightened out the twisted belt and slackened the adjustable buckle at the back, which had ridden up over the waistband of his shorts. "There, that's done it. It was only the hard metal corner of the buckle pressing into your back whenever you made a sudden movement."

"Oh, thank you, Matron," beamed Jennings, delighted at being restored once more to normal health. "It was a nasty shock when I felt it, though, I don't mind telling you. Do you think I ought to rest, and take things quietly for a few days?"

"I don't think that will be necessary, Jennings."

"Pity!" he mused. "Mr. Wilkins is going to give us a

double maths test to-morrow, to make up for missing one last Friday, and I was hoping . . ." He broke off as he caught the look of amusement in Matron's eyes. He knew from past experience that it was no good trying to hood-wink her.

He was about to ask her advice on the subject of sur-plus alarm clocks, when his glance strayed towards the fireplace; on the mantelpiece above were half a dozen birthday greetings cards, gay in colour and design.

"I say, Matron, those aren't—er—I mean, it's not *your* birthday to-day by any chance, is it?" he asked.

She admitted it with a smile.

"Gosh! I didn't know Matrons had birthdays! I mean—er—well, fancy that."

Matron's birthday! His face lighted up with inspira-tion; no need, now, to ask her advice about the trouble-some time-piece. Why, the solution was staring him in the face!

He hurried from the room, chortling with delight at his brilliant brainwave. Good old Matron! She was ever so decent, he told himself, as he trotted down the stairs. Whatever one's trouble—whether it was heads stuck in glass cases, stubbed toes, twisted-belt-buckle-itis, or even how to get rid of delicate alarm-clocks—whatever it was, she always had the remedy at her finger-tips. If ever any-one deserved a decent present for services rendered, that person was good old Matron!

No one could possibly object if the clock was given to her. Why, all the boarders would be as pleased as seventy-nine dogs with a hundred and fifty-eight tails to think they were bringing her a little happiness on such a red-letter day as this. Or would they? . . . Supposing—just *suppos-ing* that some bat-witted clodpoll voted against this bril-liant way out of their difficulties! Jennings frowned in thought. He would put the question to Darbishire—tact-fully, of course, and without mentioning any names—and see what he thought.

He found Darbishire waiting for him at the bottom of the stairs.

"How's the gout?" his friend inquired with kindly concern. "I expect Matron agreed with what I suspected, didn't she?"

"Never mind that now," Jennings answered impatiently. "I've just had a supersonic brainwave about what we can do with the clock."

"Oh, good-o: what?"

"Well, listen, Darbi. If you knew someone whom everybody liked, because they were so decent; and if this someone had a birthday, would you agree that it would be all right for someone else to give that person a birthday present, which everyone else had contributed to, because that person was so decent?"

Darbishire looked blank.

"I don't follow all this first, second and third person stuff—it's too much like French verbs," he said. "Who are all these somebodies, anyway?"

"Well, call the character with the birthday, Person A, and the character with the present going begging, Person B."

"And everybody else, characters C, D, and E, down as far as Z," Darbishire suggested brightly.

"That's right. Well, would C to Z mind if B gave A a present they'd all paid for?"

"I shouldn't think so," said Darbishire, who hadn't the slightest idea of what his friend was talking about.

"That's what I thought. All right then, Darbi. Beetle off to the Common Room at full-tilt and broadcast a special news bulletin. Tell them it's Matron's birthday to-day, and a famous, special presentation ceremony is going to take place directly after tea."

Matron was surprised when Venables and Temple knocked at her sitting-room door shortly after tea, and told her that her presence was requested in the Common Room.

When she arrived, flanked on either side by her bounding escort, she found the room packed from wall to wall with boys. In front of them stood Jennings, holding an object swathed in layers of newspaper. Mr. Carter was there too, she noticed, affecting to take no notice of the elaborate preparations that were taking place round about him.

"What's all this about my being wanted?" she asked.

Jennings stepped forward and thrust the bulky parcel into her hands.

"As it's your birthday, Matron, and because you've been so decent to us, all the chaps want me to give you this."

Matron peeled off the wrappings and looked at the gift with pleasure and surprise.

"An alarm clock; how lovely!" she exclaimed. "But you shouldn't have spent your money on me, you know."

"We didn't, Matron—or rather, we didn't *mean* to—or rather . . . Well, anyway, we hope it's what you want," Jennings finished up awkwardly.

There was no need to spoil matters, he thought, by explaining that it was the merest chance that they happened to have a present to dispose of.

The subscribers stood beaming and smiling, like proud parents at a school concert. They seemed self-conscious and just a little embarrassed by this public display of their generosity, and none of them could think of anything to say.

So Matron said: "Thank you" four times in succession, and then followed an awkward pause which lasted until Darbishire edged his way out of the throng and whispered in Jennings' ear.

"I say, what about my famous speech? I spent hours preparing it, don't forget. Of course, it's really in honour of Old Wilkie, but it'd go down just as well as a birthday speech if I altered the names round."

"Gosh, yes! I'd forgotten you were going to woffle, Darbi. You'd better do it now and get it over with."

Jennings turned to the crowd and announced: "Attention, please! I now call upon C. E. J. Darbishire to address the meeting with a few well-chosen words."

"Good old Darbi!" called Venables, and at once a thunderous burst of applause echoed round the room and shattered the atmosphere of restraint. Table-thumping and foot-stamping were added to the shouts and cheers, until the room rocked with sound. In the midst of the tumult sat Mr. Carter, smiling broadly at the noisy demonstrations going on around him. He liked to see the boys enjoying themselves!

The sound of upraised voices and thumping feet carried far beyond the walls of the Common Room. Mr. Wilkins heard the noise as he came marching along the corridor, and he thrust open the Common Room door, bristling with indignation at this display of rowdy behaviour.

Then he saw Matron holding the alarm clock . . . He saw Jennings standing beside her, and Darbishire acknowledging the applause of the crowd with a dignified bow . . . And at once Mr. Wilkins' anger melted away.

It had come as something of a shock to him, that morning, to learn from Mr. Carter that Jennings and his friends had meant no disrespect by their extraordinary behaviour during the past ten days—in fact, rather the reverse! And Mr. Wilkins had been touched by the idea of those muddle-headed boys actually feeling sorry when they thought he was leaving, and going to all that trouble to buy a present for him.

He had misjudged them. They couldn't really be so bad as he'd supposed, if they entertained such tender feelings on his behalf. Scatterbrained, certainly—but not *bad*!

He stood quietly in the doorway listening as Darbishire, tense with nervousness, cleared his throat for the famous oration.

"Matron and Gentlemen: Unaccustomed as I am to public speaking, it gives me much pleasure to be very happy to—er— . . . very happy to—er . . ."

The orator faltered. What on earth came next? For the life of him he couldn't remember. He fumbled in his pocket for his notes . . . They weren't there! He must have left them in his desk in the classroom.

He searched his brain frantically for the next well-chosen phrase . . . and then went pale with panic as he realised that every word of his carefully planned speech had fled from his mind.

He shot an appealing glance at Jennings, hoping that his friend would come to his aid. Then he gulped and stammered haltingly:

159

"Gives me much pleasure to be very happy—to—er—very happy . . . Oh, fish-hooks, I can't remember what comes next! Happy *something* . . . happy . . . happy . . ."

"Happy Birthday to you!" Jennings sang out at the top of his voice. "Happy Birthday to you!"

And then all the seventy-nine boarders and Mr. Carter joined in the song with the full force of their lungs:

> *"Happy Birthday, dear Matron,*
> *Happy Birthday to you!"*

As the last notes died away, the sudden nerve-shattering ear-splitting shrilling of the alarm bell broke on the air.

Matron leapt like a wild gazelle and nearly dropped the clock: then she recovered and broke into a peal of laughter. Soon everybody was laughing with her, and the noise swelled to a fantastic symphony of mirth.

Mr. Wilkins didn't actually laugh out loud. But he was smiling inwardly as he closed the door and made his way along the corridor.

"Silly little boys," he muttered to himself, though not unkindly. "*Silly* little boys!"